THE TIMBER SHED

ELLE HYDE

PublishAmerica
Baltimore

Softcover 9781462665198
PUBLISHED BY PUBLISHAMERICA, LLLP
www.publishamerica.com
Baltimore

Printed in the United States of America

This book is lovingly dedicated to my husband, Mark.

This book started six years ago after a visit to Reims, France. The story may not have been told if not for his tireless encouragement, care giving, and support.

Thank you for making all of the sacrifices you have made to keep me writing. I love you.

CHAPTER ONE
A SAFE PLACE

Jacquemart sat motionless recalling his earliest memories of the timber shed. The weathered brown rough-cut timber walls of the small shed had always offered him security and a sense of comfort. The symbolic womb was a place where he could briefly escape the taunting, condemning torment of his life. His conscious thoughts were dissociative and his unconscious thoughts were consumed with violence. The demons within his head were somehow quieted and shut out when he was in the timber shed.

Jacquemart was most comforted when he sat in the corner of the small space that offered little to no light. Light was an intruder that peered through the cracks of the boards, invading his solace. Surprisingly, when Jacquemart was inside of the seven by eight foot room, he did not feel caged in, even though he was a large man. The small window had been boarded up since he was a child. The blood stains, no longer red but now a dark brown, still reminded him of the countless times he beat his head on the splintered wood in an attempt to rid the demons from his mind. He never understood the dichotomy of the timber shed. He hated having come into the world imprisoned, although he sought comfort from a room no larger than the same prison cell where his mother had given birth.

The common feeling of helplessness hung over his psyche like a dark shadow that could never escape.

As he crouched in the corner with his arms tucked underneath his knees, he stared into the darkness, yet he was surrounded by daylight and lush green woods.

Most who saw Jacquemart perceived him to be confident, but quiet; handsome, but weathered looking. The vulnerable side of Jacquemart, the man who sat alone, so vulnerable in the small, dark shed, was unseen by everyone. The creases in his brow line now showed his turmoil. His large brown eyes appeared vacuous, concealing any sign of emotion behind the handsome edifice. His shaved black hair matched the razor stubble left on his chin. His full lips atrophied to form a smile.

Jacquemart thought about the time and knew he had to motivate himself to meet his party. He carried out this impending chore as a form of catharsis. He was acutely aware of the cycle of birth, nurturing, allowing one to go free, and the pearls that were met with that freedom. He played out life's cycle of birth through death every day. He was going to choose one of the young females to be sacrificed today. He always chose females. Jacquemart felt that females did not deserve to be the givers of life. The responsibilities that were associated with the ability to give birth were wasted on this sex. This feeling of intense anger stemmed from his own abandonment, handed down by his mother and stepmother.

He stood up, took in a deep breath, and shifted his neck to the left and then to right, readjusting his skeletal frame, his neck cracking from stiffness due to the unnatural sitting position he assumed while in the timber shed. It took a mere three steps for him to move through the doorway and into the light of the day. The rain had ceased and the mist was heavy in the air. The leaves hung low, heavy from the water that rested on them. He did not notice the drops of rain that slowly dripped down his forehead as his head brushed against the leaves.

The woods were as much a part of him as the blood that pulsed through his body. He found peace, comfort, and the only sense of belonging he had ever experienced while in the large, vast woods that surrounded his château.

Jacquemart had been left the 200-acre family estate by his father. The Dartmounts had a 400-year aristocratic presence in the North East Champagne region of France, dating back to the 1600s.

Jacquemart had the family heritage schooled into him, whereas his father had it bred into him. Jacquemart had to be schooled on how to be superior due to birth circumstances, but for Jacquemart, therein lay the problem.

Despite his training, schooling, and education, he could not convince himself of the superiority complex that came attached to the Dartmount name. He was raised as a Dartmount: Jacquemart Dartmounts III, to be exact. He was sole heir to a diminished line of French aristocrats. In fact, he was the last male Dartmount, and in truth, he was a bastard.

He reached the pickup truck and opened the door. He turned the engine on and drove into the woods along the small narrow paths made by his truck on a daily basis. He looked into the rearview mirror, back at the timber shed. As it faded into the background, he turned his attention forward, stared straight out onto the path, and sighed.

"It is time," he said to himself, "Time to get the boar."

CHAPTER TWO
COUNTRY PATE

The small silver Porsche stopped inches short of hitting the brick wall. The door swung open and out jumped Piper, wrestling with her purse while trying to lock the car and grab the handle of the restaurant's back door. As she stepped inside of the building, the metal door slammed shut behind her, locking out the sounds of the back alley, allowing her to focus on the new commotion awaiting her. The kitchen was busy and noisy. She glanced down at the time on her cell phone to see how late she was in actuality. She was preparing herself for the wrath of Nico.

She opened the door to her office and placed her purse behind the desk. She took off her pumps and slipped out of her skirt and into a set of kitchen whites and clogs. She quickly pulled her hair back and tied it before she closed the door and walked back down the hallway.

She stopped before entering the main kitchen and grabbed a fresh, clean apron from the shelf. She took in a long, deep breath as she fumbled with the apron strings and tied them into a small, perfect bow at the front of her waist.

She stepped into the kitchen and there was her husband, Nico. He was waiting for Piper that morning to assist him in preparing a wild boar for a private booking. Nico had a staff of 12 male chefs, but that particular morning, Nico depended on Piper to help him, although she was not the most qualified for the job. Piper specialized in pastries, while Nico was the head chef.

As she walked back to the prep area of the large commercial kitchen, gleaming and shining with meticulous commercial opulence, she found Nico restive, moody, and already at work.

"Piper, you're late," he screamed at her.

She took a deep breath and walked toward him, holding out her hands with her signature smile placed dramatically upon her lips.

Unto all, Piper was beautiful. She had long, full auburn hair, deep lipid green eyes, and large full lips that expressed her efflorescent personality.

"Nico, my love, I am not that late," she whispered in his ear as he worked. Nico did not look up.

"There is no such thing as 'not so late'. Late is late, Piper," he replied.

Nico was intense, confident, and condescending. Despite what many thought to be negative traits, Piper fell in love with these qualities. Nico swept her off her feet with his debonair presence. She saw the world as freely as the affection that flowed from her spirit. Nico saw the world as meticulous and intense as his being.

Nico worked with his head down, bent over, cutting apart the dead animal. The 125-pound animal lay spread out on top of the prep table, head intact, viscous tusks pointing upward in a semi-circle, black, course, bristled hair matted with dried blood. Boars were ugly animals and gave Piper an ill feeling when she had to work around them. Preparing wild boar was a difficult job that consisted of removing the head, ears, legs, and hooves, filleting the meat, and then cooking down the head and bones.

After Nico's last statement, Piper decided to assist without commenting. She stood to the side and a step behind the chef. Piper and Nico had married three years earlier and had started the restaurant only a few months after their marriage. Nico Blanche was a renowned French chef. The restaurant, Petite Piper, was named after her. Nico was the head chef and Piper managed the business and the pastry kitchen. When the two had met, Nico had just sold his business due to his poor management of finances.

The shiny, perfectly honed blade of the meat cleaver slammed down on the large butcher-block table, separating the ears of the boar from the head. Piper jumped at the sound.

Nico raised the blade and slammed it down a second time, precisely and assiduously severing the head from the base of the spine. Piper jumped again at the point where the blade hit the wooden table.

"Piper, take the head," he yelled at her.

Piper picked up the head, avoiding looking into the glazed-over eye that stared seemingly at her. She dreaded helping Nico with this job. After placing the head in the properly labeled garbage container, she turned and washed her hands in the large sink.

By the time Piper turned around, Nico had removed the head from the garbage and placed it in the large skillet that was on the stove adjacent to the prep room.

"Piper, the ears," he snapped at her.

She returned quickly to scoop up the ears. Moving quickly, she placed the ears in the skillet, her hands once again bloody. Without thinking, she wiped them off on her now unclean apron.

"Damn, I have to get a clean apron," she said aloud once she realized what she had done.

The evident tension between the two was thick. Piper was acutely aware that Nico was irritated with the fact that she was again dilatory. She felt compelled to address the subject, as the tacit mood between them was embarrassing to her.

"I am sorry I am late Nico." She spoke as though she was a schoolgirl apologizing to the head master. "My afternoon was very chaotic." She continued to weave an excuse that would defuse him.

She was anxious and his vituperative demeanor was causing her stress. She noticed her fingernails as she was ringing her fingers with her apron.

"Damn it, I have blood underneath my nails," she thought to herself. She looked up and smiled coyly at Nico. He was unaware that the manicure was the reason for her tardiness.

Nico was consumed by his work. He did not notice that he had caused such undue stress to Piper. Nico had this affect on most of the kitchen staff. His concentration and talent was so intense that he spoke little while working, causing a tense work environment. They never had a lack of applications, however; working for The Blanche's was a large stepping-stone in the culinary industry.

"Piper, I need you here on Thursdays at 3:00. We have been over this a million times. I do not care to hear your excuses. Now, come give me a kiss and go about your day."

He spoke while skillfully and slowly moving the blade of the large filleting knife between the boar's skin and muscle. He worked as if what he was doing was rudimentary, when the truth to the matter was that filleting the skin and the meat of a wild boar was arduous and required great concentration.

"Before you go, hand me that bin, please."

Piper had made no attempt to leave the room, and was all too familiar with Nico's acerbic mannerisms. This was his polite cue for her to leave the room.

"Alright," she replied, as could not help feeling a warm glow when she looked at him deep in concentration and so adroit. Piper saw a soft side to Nico that no one else could see. His short commands were not rude in Piper's eyes. She looked past all the rough, abrupt tones and heard a soft, loving man who was misunderstood because he was a victim to his intense concentration and talent.

She moved quickly to grab the garbage can and placed it close to him. He slid the bloody, black, bristled pelt into the bin.

"Voila," he said this time as he paused to look up at her and smile.

Piper leaned over and kissed him quickly on his lips.

"Now, move aside so I can filet the meat."

This comment signaled that the brief compassionate second had passed. During that same second when Nico had glanced up at Piper to ask her to move, his knife had slipped, skimming his knuckle.

"Piper, move out of my light. Look what you have caused."

It was not so much that Nico blamed her for his carelessness but that the kiss meant something to her that he did not feel. She sharply replied, "Nico, if you do not know how to use a knife after receiving a Michelin star, all the light in Philadelphia won't help you."

She took much of his ordering and minimizing of her self-worth, but beyond that, there was a thin line, and when Nico crossed it, she could feel their love slipping away.

"Go to your little pastry workshop and finish tonight's desserts!" he ordered her.

"Piss off, Nico!" She called back at him as she turned and walked away.

"He can be such a dick," she said to herself as she walked through the kitchen to the pastry section. "Let him dispose of his own freakin' boar," she added in closing.

By the time she reached the pastry kitchen, she was over the entire incident. Piper was the exact working opposite of Nico. She spoke often to her staff, joked, and smiled. Her pastry chefs were happy and relaxed.

"Hello, boys," she called out to her two assistants as the sound of the large mixer hummed over the sound of the peripheral kitchen banter. The two assistants were already placing the finishing touches on the evening's desserts.

After a few hours quickly passed, Piper slipped away to have a glass of wine. She left a few final instructions for her chefs and walked through the back corridor to the back office. She shared this office with Nico. As she approached the door, it swung open unexpectedly, brushing past her nose. She stepped back quickly.

"Oooh, excuse me," she said as one of the young new servers burst out, pushing past her with obvious discontent.

The opened door revealed Nico sitting at his desk. "Close the door, Piper," he called out.

"What was that all about?" she asked.

"This young jackass fucks up the orders, pisses of the guests, and fucks me off. He is a worthless piece of shit," Nico mumbled as he pulled a small hand wrapped cigarette out of his locked desk drawer. Nico had been making his own clove cigarettes since she met him.

"Nico, we cannot afford to go through another server. He is new and young. Give him some guidance and time,"

Piper tried to reason with him. As she spoke to him, he lit his cigarette took long, slow drags of it.

His drawer had remained open. There, in the front section by the paperclips was a small baggy of fine white powder.

"Is that was I think it is?" she pointed and asked him. As the business manager, Piper was the one putting out the fires from Nico's bad behavior. She did not condone drug use in the kitchen, but the truth of the matter was that many of the head chefs could not work the grueling hours without small pick-me-ups; it was very common in the business.

Nico did not answer her rhetorical question.

Piper grabbed the corked bottle of wine sitting on her desk and poured it into the glass resting beside it. As she poured it, she laughed to herself, "One vice for another, I guess." She took a sip and continued to speak, trying to focus back on the business of running their business. "Nico, do not dismiss him yet. Let Adam work with him. We cannot afford to turn over another server."

Nico smoked his cigarette while Piper drank her red wine, each sitting at their desk trying to momentarily enjoy a relaxed break, each with their own vice and form of recreation. They stared straight ahead at the office door.

"Fine, you manage Adam to work with the piece of shit, as long as he does not screw up another order or piss off me or one of my chefs," Nico said after a minute had passed in silence. He sat back in his chair, placed his hands behind his head, and stretched casually.

"And you, what is your value today, Piper?" he looked at her without any hint of sarcasm.

Curious as this his behavior was, she replied, "Nico, don't quiz me. I completed the shopping order; managed the restaurant and the house. I forgot; this is in addition to cooking here." She looked him in the eyes and waited to see where this conversation would go.

"Pour me a glass of the pinot noir behind you, please," he replied with a smile.

"You are an ass, Nico Blanche," she replied as she got up and walked over to him. She was happy to see that his response was light-hearted and not meant to incite an argument this time.

She spun him around in his chair and then turned to pour him a glass of wine from the uncorked bottle. She grabbed the glass that was on his desk. As she began to pour the wine into it, she noticed pink lipstick on the rim. Her gut instinct nagged at her as she worked to control her natural response to interrogate him. She knew from experience that this reaction did not work, and he would merely lie. She would have to wait until she saw an opportunity to question him as to the woman who had shared a glass of wine with him in his office the night before, when she had gone home early, at his request.

She turned and placed the glass in front of him, just beyond his reach, causing him to move out of his relaxed position to get it.

"Is my trip planned yet?" he asked.

"No, Nico. Have you planned the trip yet?" she snapped back. "I have not had a single moment of time to think let alone plan your stupid trip. Isn't that Anne Marie's job?" she added before concluding, "I have to go back to work."

"What has got into you?" he replied.

"The usual, Nico," she said as she drank down the rest of her wine, which normally would have been savored in several slow drinks.

He did not understand her comment, but did not push the subject.

She walked out and closed the door behind her, leaving Nico in the room by himself. As she walked down the hall back to the kitchen, she passed the hostess, who also worked as a personal assistant to them both.

"Angie, will you please see to it that Nico's trip to France is booked. He is in his office; you can go get the details from him. Tell him I don't have time."

"Certainly, Piper," she replied as she walked toward the office.

The trip to France had been planned for months. Nico was asked to cook with a good friend of his at a charity event. Piper was not going to attend, although it just so happened to be in the town where they had met. She thought it could be a romantic weekend, but Nico convinced her that they both could not leave the restaurant at this time.

"I wonder who is sharing wine with Nico this time," Piper thought to herself as she took off her apron, threw it in the hamper, and pushed through the back door. She was not scheduled to leave, but the second she made the decision to ask Angie to plan the trip, she decided it was time to go home.

She walked to her waiting car with anxiety and stress, much how she had entered the restaurant hours before.

CHAPTER THREE
ONE'S FATE

A small hand-painted wooden sign sticking out of the ground in front of a large metal gate displayed the words "Parcel Number 24."

This was a walled 30-acre piece of forest owned by the Dartmounts. Jacquemart Dartmount stood in the drizzling rain sorting through the wet keys in search of the one that would open the lock to the gateway.

Jacquemart raised wild boar and red stag. He raised them from birth to be let out onto one of the three parcels of land so hunters could kill them for a fee. This was an old aristocratic hobby used by King Henry VIII and Napoleon. Egomaniacal rulers and aristocrats would hunt small game in small penned-in areas so they would be assured of a kill. Some of the parcels of land would consume only seven to ten acres. Within the walls of the parceled land, the servants would wait until the lord of the estate drew near; then, they would throw out a wild boar, hare, or red stag. The animal would appear maybe within a mere ten yards from the huntsmen. The walled grounds prevented the animal from escaping. It was considered an embarrassment if the king, lord, or prince returned to the manor or château empty-handed. This custom was taught to Jacquemart Dartmount by his father, who would take him on hunts on the very same parcel when he was a young boy.

Jacquemart had the merits to do the hunting, but found himself leasing his land and helpless animals to the rich. This day, he was to release one young wild boar—one of the boars that he had helped birth. As he opened the gate and walked back to the truck, he thought about the animal that was kicking and squealing inside the large metal carrier hauled behind the truck.

He recalled the difficulty, and soon, the ultimate demise of the animal.

"He and I share the same life," he thought as he drove toward the small pen.

Once within the grounds, he was met by a group of hunters awaiting his arrival. As they stood in a group, smoking, laughing, and drinking cuvée from a glass bottle, their breath appeared as a puff of white smoke due to the cold, damp air.

Jacquemart backed the trailer up against a small wooden door that had a pulley and rope attached to the top. He jumped out of the truck with a long tool that had a hook on its end. He walked back to the trailer and placed two pieces of board along each side of it, closing any gaps between the back of the trailer and the wooden gate. He jumped up and onto of the trailer, catching the attention of the hunters.

One pointed to him and their conversation ceased as they focused on Jacquemart. He athletically jumped down onto his stomach and reached down to the handle on the back door of the trailer. He lifted it up and slid himself back, opening the door. The squealing of the boar drew cheers from the hunters. The sound of the hooves kicking against the metal door of the trailer displayed the aggression of the animal.

Jacquemart jumped down off the trailer and walked over to a set of wooden steps that led to a small platform above the wall and the small wooden door. He ascended the steps and pulled the rope to raise the wooden door. The boar did not find the small opening; instead it ran back into the trailer.

The hunters booed and laughed, seeding well-known feelings of insecurity within Jacquemart. He jumped off the trailer and grabbed the hunter's hook that lay on the ground. He moved the board and walked into the pen and after the boar. He pinned the young female boar into the corner, slipped the hook over her neck, and twisted the handle, tightening the hook. He dragged her, fighting for her life as she snarled and snorted, instinctually fighting for her existence. Jacquemart was the victor; he emerged from the back of the truck fueled by anger, dragging the squealing, snorting boar behind him. He lifted his boot and kicked the doors of the trailer closed. He dragged the boar over to the door of the make-shift pen and released the hook with a twist of the handle. The boar escaped from Jacquemart and into the walled parcel of land. There, she started to run. She would continue to run until she was exhausted and cornered, outnumbered by hounds and unable to defend herself. Today, this boar would meet her fate by being speared through the neck or torn apart by hounds.

Jacquemart, once again, walked up the wooden steps to the rope holding the gate. He was acting out the same maneuvers his father had done in front of him countless times. As a young boy, he would imagine the guillotine slamming down upon a fragile, thin neck, severing it, when his father would release the door from the pulley, allowing it to slam shut. The rusty wheel spun, unraveling the rope until the final bang of the heavy wood against the base stone jarred him back to reality. He allowed the twine to slip through his hands as the gate slammed shut, sealing the boar's fate.

Jacquemart turned and walked toward the group of men. One of the men stepped forward and held out his hand. Jacquemart did not reach out and shake it. He ignored the man completely.

"If you want to go inside, I will release the hounds," he said. This particular booking rented the grounds, bought the boar, if killed, by the pound, and rented his hounds. Jacquemart's hounds were prized. They were well-trained, experienced hunters from a hundred-year-old family-owned bloodline. Hunters both from the country and abroad traveled to these grounds to hunt with Jacquemart's hounds. They guaranteed a kill to any hunter using them. Jacquemart trained them from a very early age to lust after the blood of the boars.

"Men, to the hunt," said the lead huntsman.

They all raised their hands in the air and cheered as they passed the bottle.

Jacquemart opened the gate. They walked through it and then stopped, waiting for Jacquemart to release his hounds. He walked back to his trailer and removed the wooden side fencing. He hopped into the trailer and once inside, opened a second door that contained 20 hounds, one of which was CeCeine, Jacquemart's beloved hound.

The brown, black, and white hounds ran out of the trailer, barking and nipping at one another. A large "D" was carved into each dog's fur, proudly representing the family name.

CeCeine ran out of the trailer, onto the ground, and was the first to pick up the scent of the boar. She led the pack as they all ran through the opening and into the woods. The sound of the barking pack grew faint as they followed CeCeine deeper into the woods.

The hunters prepared their spears and set off into the woods. One of the youngest hounds was off sniffing on his own, away from the pack. Jacquemart picked up a long seven-foot crop and snapped it at the young hound. The dog yelped and ran through the gate, chasing after the rest of the pack.

Jacquemart closed the gate and walked back to the old, dented pickup truck. Once inside, he reached over and opened a flask that housed rare cognac. He drank the expensive liquor from an old tarnished flask that had the Dartmount crest on the front.

Jacquemart did not think twice about the nominal fee being paid to him. It was exceedingly outbalanced by the value of the cognac that he was drinking from the seventeenth century flask.

The Dartmount family fell into ruins at the time of his father's death. His stepmother's lover devised the plan to rent out the family's land for income. She willingly went along, as he was much younger and she feared losing his companionship. The once proud historical château stood derelict, surrounded by overgrown gardens. Jacquemart was raised as the caretaker of the four parcels of various sizes used for the rented hunting grounds. In addition to the income from the hunts, Jacquemart leased out 100 acres of prime vineyard to the local champagne houses. He did not care for, cultivate, or participate in the process, but was afforded the income and an allotted age of champagne from the famed Dartmount wine cellar. This same wine cellar housed the rare champagnes and cognacs that he dismissively drank on a daily basis. The wine caves were built out of the original limestone walls that were once enveloped by the sea. The history and value were misplaced with Jacquemart, who merely saw the château, alcohol, and land as a shard of glass left in him from his tormented childhood.

Jacquemart started the truck and drove through the misty woods on the meandering road until the large limestone château appeared in front of him like a figment of his vivid nightmares. Jacquemart drove through the crested gate and to the back of the house where the kennels were located. As the truck approached, the hounds heard the sound and reacted with enthusiasm. The collection of hounds barking rang out like a chorus of bells, each one barking at a different pitch.

"It is time to feed the hounds," he said to himself as he pulled up to the pandemonium. To many, the rancorous noise would be unnerving, but it comforted Jacquemart.

As he approached the cages, the dogs growled and mauled one another, fighting for dominance over the pack. As he entered the cage, the animals moved away from him in an instinctual effort to avoid pain. He saw their lives very much as his own.

CHAPTER FOUR
ON THE OTHER END

He walked quickly to the wooden watchtower that sat at the end of the fence line. He climbed up the timber ladder and into the small wooden structure. A table, chair, bottle of wine, and cigarettes sat in the center of the room. A large cutout on the sides and front served as windows. Large wooden shutters rose from the bottom and were secured on top to serve as protection from the harsh winter storms. Jacquemart stood at the front window listening. He remained inert, straining his ears to hear that soothing sound, the barking of the hounds. To Jacquemart, the pandemonium of the yelping, growling clan was a beautiful sound. A trained huntsman knows exactly where the pack is by the hounds' voices. He heard CeCeine's bark, then the echoed bark of the pack as she sought out the prey. Jacquemart became aroused by the offering of the prey. He stood listening to the dogs' frantic calls to one another. He unzipped his pants and released his erect penis from his trousers. He began to rub his penis to the imagined sound of the boar's heartbeat, pounding, thumping, throbbing. He heard the sound of a living creature afraid for its life. The rhythm of a frantic heartbeat was the timing he used to masturbate. The thought of the blood pulsing and surging through the fear-consumed animal brought him closer to climax, as he kept the same rhythm. His heart pounded. His adrenaline rose. As he envisioned the hounds surrounding the animal, he stroked himself harder and faster. As the heartbeat of fear set the rhythm, so did he. He imagined the boar paralyzed with fear. He envisioned the hounds striking at the legs of the boar. He leaned over and placed his left hand against the wall of the wooden framed structure, bracing his tense, muscular body, as he knew he was about to climax.

The dogs grabbed at the legs, breaking the bones of the fragile, fatigued boar. As the boar fell, the dogs lunged forward. CeCeine's jaws penetrated the throat of the frantic animal that lay wounded, bracing for death.

Jacquemart climaxed the moment he saw the vision in his mind of CeCeine's powerful jaws piercing the throat of the boar. He could hear the silencing of the animal's heart. The hunt was done. His climax was complete. Jacquemart fell back and sat on the wooden stool, allowing his heart to slow down. He breathed in the surrounding air slowly, savoring the moment. He pulled his pants up and zipped up his trousers. With limp muscles, he sat in quiet satisfaction of the release. His moment was soon interrupted by the intrusion of the huntsman's call.

"Come weigh the boar. The hunt is done," he called out across the small two-way radio. "I will meet you at the timber shed," replied Jacquemart.

He stood up and descended the small fortress tower. He got into his truck and drove to the front gate. He opened the iron gate and allowed it to swing open as he got back into his truck and drove through it.

He thought to himself, "There is no longer a need for imprisonment. The prisoner has been released from its life of torment."

His mood quickly turned as he began to envy the death of the boar. He thought, "To be freed from imprisonment with such drama would be beautiful."

The huntsmen stood surrounding the boar, cheering, drinking, and laughing with one another.

Jacquemart asked one of the huntsmen, "Where is the boar?" He was consumed with unbridled excitement and anticipation to see the kill.

"There it comes, now," the huntsman said as he pointed back toward the woods.

Two men were carrying the boar on a rail with its front and back legs bound together. The head bobbed back with each step as its warm body dripped blood through the woods leading back to the place of its demise.

The pack of hounds barked and snapped at the dead boar, licking the bloody drops as it was carried to the timber shed.

Jacquemart screamed out, "Protect the carcass." He noticed CeCeine was not with the pack of dogs. He placed his cracked fingers to his lips and whistled a loud, piercing pitch. Within seconds, CeCeine ran from behind the pack over to her master, proud of her accomplishment.

"Good CeCeine," he said as he gave her a single stroke on the head.

Jacquemart reached into his shirt pocket and pulled out a wrinkled pack of cigarettes. He placed one on his bottom lip and lit it as he walked over to the scale that hung outside the timber shed.

"Drop it there," he said as he pointed to the ground, never making eye contact with the hunters; his eyes remained fixed on the dead boar.

The hunters dropped the dead boar to the ground.

"CeCeine!" he called out with force and authority. The large tan, white, and black dog ran to his side. She was bloodied, wet, and muddy. "Good CeCeine," he praised her as he stroked her head. She looked at her master with ardor and pride.

The huntsmen dragged the boar by its tusks over to the large metal scale that hung from the tree. Jacquemart reached up, pulled the cigarette from his sternly defined lips, and flicked it to the ground. He walked over to it stamping it out in passing, but not with intent. He grabbed the boar with one hand. The two huntsmen it took to move it to the scale stood aside as he yanked the limp body upwards impaling it on the large rusted hook at the end of the rod. The hand of the scale moved upwards, then backwards, forward, back, and then rested on 100 lbs.

"It's 45.36 kilos. You owe me 200 Euros," he spoke aloud to the crowd of hunters. They all reached into their pockets and counted out the bills to meet the fee.

"Do you want the meat or can I feed it to the hounds? The legs and innards are reserved for the hounds. You may have the head if you wish," he questioned the group of men.

The organizer of the hunt stepped forward and handed Jacquemart a wad of bills.

"Two hundred Euros. I want the head; keep the rest. Stay and have a drink with us. We must toast your hounds. We figure the hunt lasted one hour. That is a quick but lively hunt. Your reputation is well deserved," he said to Jacquemart.

"I will cut off the head and gut the boar. While my dogs are resting and savoring the moment, I will have one drink with you," replied Jacquemart. He did not acknowledge the compliment. He did not need the fatuous flattery. He knew his hounds were prized, he knew his land was the best, and his reputation was impeccable. He did not need adulation from a peasant hunter.

The organizer walked into the timber shed, and moments later, descended with an uncorked bottle of red Bordeaux. He handed the bottle to Jacquemart for first tasting.

"To the hunt," he proclaimed.

"To the hunt," the others called out.

Jacquemart grasped the bottle that was held high in the air, moved it to his lips, and took a long and slow drink. As he moved the bottle away from his lips, red wine dripped from the sides of his mouth. He did not instinctually wipe it away.

"To the climax of the hunt." He handed the organizer the bottle and walked away from the men.

He walked over to the sacrificial boar and lifted the bloodied body with only three legs left attached up and off the hook. It dropped to the ground with a thud.

He reached toward the brown leather belt that holstered a large gutting knife. The knife and the belt had been handed down to him by his father. They were part of the short memories he had of his father before he died. He spent only five years with the stern paternal figure before his succumbed to death. His father instilled a large sense of pride in him within their fleeting father-son relationship.

"With pride, Jacquemart, shall you be caretaker of the land and château. You will be responsible one day for carrying on the Dartmount name, and with great pride shall you take that privilege." He could still hear his father speaking these words. Jacquemart realized he was standing still staring at the knife while he heard his father's words resonate in his head. The knife was masculine and garish. The handle was made from a large red stag horn and the blade was forged steel with the family's crest etched in the metal. The blade was sharp and rigged. The leather holster was weathered and old, but well cared for and oiled. The metal case of the blade was made of brass. From an early age, Jacquemart had been taught how to care for the holster, case, and blade. He did so every other day, whether it needed tending or not.

He moved toward the carcass and lifted the blade eye level. He plunged the blade into the animal at the neck and forced it downward in a deep, vigorous, rigid movement, cutting through the tough thick skin of the animal. The course, wiry, black hair with whitish pink flesh was flooded with thick red blood. As the large incision enveloped the length of the animal's body, Jacquemart spread the incision open. The dogs stood inches away sniffing the air. Some snapped at one another, fighting over the territory. CeCeine stood still and faithful beside Jacquemart. She knew better than to lunge.

One of the younger more immature dogs overstepped its boundary and lunged toward the open incision. Jacquemart caught the hound on the nose. *"BACK!"* he yelled as he struck the hound, forcing it to step back into submission.

Disappointed, he stopped and stood still. CeCeine looked up at her large, stern, and imposing master. She shrunk down instinctually, sensing his anger. *"You worthless hound, how dare you make me look vituperative to your haste,"* he thought to himself.

He reached once again for his holster. The older hounds in the pack sat or shrunk down, knowing the impending, imminent wrath. He pulled out the black leather whip. He took two steps back and raised the whip above his head, snapping it quickly with massive strength toward the young hound who had usurped his authority.

The end of the whip snapped forward, catching the young hound on the nose. The dog cried out, not so much from pain but from fear. His nose separated and began to bleed. The others in the pack stepped two, if not three, steps back. The young dog lowered himself to the floor and rolled over on his back in a submissive position.

The huntsmen looked on as they drank, smoked, and told tales of the narrow escapes when the boar lunged at them with its tusks. Their banter was momentarily disrupted by the commotion. The group glanced over at the pack of hounds, but was too interested in themselves and their masculine bonding session. To them, the disciplining whip striking one of the dogs was mundane and meaningless.

Jacquemart stepped forward and stared at the animals. None would make eye contact with him. This was sufficient. He grabbed the end of the whip and rolled it back up, placing it back into the leather holster. He snapped the leather band around it.

He knelt over and reached into the boar. He ripped out the stomach and threw it toward CeCeine. This was her reward. The others ran toward the bloodied organ, but she snarled and snipped at the others. They soon became aware of their standing. Jacquemart worked quickly now, as he knew the others were becoming contentious.

He cut around the boar's head and then stood up, placing his foot on the shoulder of the carcass and his left hand on the snout. He snapped the head upward, breaking the spine and freeing the head from the body.

With one hand, he lifted the head by the tusk and walked back over to the hunters. The dogs descended upon the remains of the boar with wild instinctual passion. They ripped, fought, snapped, barked, and tugged at the organs. One of the hounds snapped off the back leg and ran with it away from the pack over to a small tree, where it lay down gnawing at the severed hind leg. There, the two remaining legs soon met the same fate.

As Jacquemart met the group of hunters, he pushed through their circle and threw the head in the center.

"Bon Souvenir. Here is your memory." He walked away, back to his truck, where he would sit until the hounds had had their fill of the boar. He was pleased that the hunters had allowed his hounds to devour the meat. More often than not, he would take the meat and allow the hounds to consume the innards. The hunters always wanted the head as the trophy of their masculine superiority over the inferior. His hounds could use the meat as a means of motivation for the next hunt that was scheduled a week from this date. As the dogs dispersed to lie down and gnaw on the remaining bones, all that was left of the boar was the skin. Jacquemart got of his truck and walked over to the mere remains. He picked up the pelt and threw it in the back of the truck.

He got in and started the engine.

"Men, it is time to get off my land," he called out. The hunters looked over at him, laughing and celebrating. They walked toward the front gate. Jacquemart followed slowly behind them in his truck, herding them off his land. He whistled out the window and called, "CeCeine, come!" She quickly dropped the task at hand and ran after the truck that was slowly moving toward the gate. The others that lagged behind were summoned by CeCeine, who organized the pack. There were always one or two hounds that stayed in the woods. Jacquemart would go back after the stray one or two, and it was a certainty that they would not repeat their insolence.

When the truck moved to leave and CeCeine called, all were compelled to follow. That was the order. As Jacquemart threw the hounds into the back of the carrier and closed the door, pushing all of them into the cubicle, he felt solace. Birth, struggle, sacrifice, passion, and death; his vision of the cycle of life was carried out today. He felt privileged to orchestrate, manipulate, and view the drama that was his life and destiny.

CHAPTER FIVE
UNEXPECTED GIFTS

As Nico kicked the back door open with his kitchen work boot, the files stuffed under his arm fell to the ground, spilling the papers onto the wet, dirty cement of the back parking lot. "Putain de merde!" he screamed out in frustration.

He was losing the battle as he wrestled with the boxes, bags, and files that he was carrying. It was merely 7:00 A.M., but his arrival at this hour was required if he was to go with Piper to France and feel confident that the restaurant would run smoothly in their absence.

As he entered the kitchen, the early staff was already busy preparing for the day. His sous chef ran to his aid.

"Here, let me help you, Chef." The young chef took the boxes from his arms.

Nico turned and went back outside to gather the contents of the file. Marco, the sous chef, placed the boxes on the island in the back kitchen and opened the back door to assist him in gathering the scattered paper.

"Ah, it is going to be a bad day, Marco, as you can already see." Nico did not look up but spoke to him from a bent down position, mumbling, "J'essaie de bosser, connard."

All of the chefs in the kitchen were accustomed to Chef's mumbling and strange dialect. Nico was born in France to French parents. He had visited the States only three times in his life prior to meeting Piper. He did not find the celebrity status in America that he experienced in France. He degraded Americans for this, sarcastically calling them "bons vivants," suggesting that they lacked a sophisticated palate. Piper loved France, but her parents lived in Philadelphia. During the tenure of their marriage, both of her beloved parents had passed away, causing much loneliness for Piper.

"Chef, there was a bag left on the back kitchen island. It looked like a gift." Marco was nervous and made it elusive that he did not intrude on the chef's personal property. "I did not open it. I assumed it was meant for you. When I got here, it was left on the prep room island." Marco did not make eye contact with Nico. "I was the first employee to arrive here this morning, so it must have been left from the night before."

"My day gets better," said Nico, acknowledging Marco for the first time with eye contact, brushing the long graying brown bangs from his eyes, revealing a shine to his normally intense facial expression.

"We do not know who it is from?" Nico asked again.

Marco replied, "I did not want to open the note card; I can guarantee it is not for me."

Nico noticed a degree of agitation that was abnormal for Marco who was consistently shy. Although Marco lacked confidence as a man, he was an immensely talented chef who had a positive career ahead of him. Marco started working with Nico after a brief stint in the kitchen when another head chef and one of Nico's chefs swapped positions for two weeks. At the time, Marco was working in a famed restaurant in Las Vegas. Once he proved himself worthy to Nico and Nico asked him to stay on, he was eager to leave his job. Nico recognized his talent and wanted him to be loyal to his restaurants. Any aspiring chef would not pass up the opportunity to work with Nico, despite his well-known temper tantrums and abusive mannerisms.

Nico stood up and pushed the collected files to Marco hastily. Marco grabbed the folder and obediently followed him back into the kitchen. Marco would not carry on with his duties until released by Chef.

Nico walked toward the stainless steel island that was untouched and shining due to the work of the cleaning crew the night before. On the island sat a metallic gold bag with black tissue paper decoratively placed on the inside reflected in the metal. Marco did not utter a word as Nico reached into the bag and pulled out a small note card. He opened the envelope and read it:

I thought you could use this now that your old one is stained. I close my eyes and dream of the next time we are together. I get wet just thinking about you.

Yours,

Nicole

He picked up the bag by the hemp string handles and quickly walked to his office clutching the note card.

He called out to Marco as he walked away, "Carry on."

"Is it from Piper?" he replied in a rare act of personal acknowledgement.

Nico kept walking without answering him. The thought of Nicole's young, soft, voluptuous body aroused him. As he approached his office, he fumbled for the keys in the front pocket of his chef pants. He opened the door and closed it behind him, locking it from inside with no chance of intrusion from the reality of the bustling kitchen.

He did not immediately reach into the bag to discover its contents. First, he walked over to the chair and sat down. He leaned back and smiled as wide as his mouth would permit. If his ego could be measured by space, his was infinite. He glanced at the bag and paused for another moment before opening it. He made sure to revel in the moment and reminisce about the last time he and Nicole were together. He became aroused at the vision of her young toned frame bent over his office desk, baring her round, firm ass. His sexual replay was then interrupted when he recalled that Piper had knocked at the door less than five minutes following his orgasm. He redirected his thoughts back to Nicole.

Nico was at a time in his life when the risk and thrill of sex with a woman two decades his junior, in his office, with dozens of his employees in the restaurant, and Piper moving about made him feel powerful and liberated. Otherwise, he felt dead and trapped in the mundane banality of his marriage. This was unacceptable for such a passionate man.

He did not spoil this particular moment with extended thoughts of Piper and their faltering relationship. He was too egomaniacal to contemplate the furtiveness of his actions and the ramifications of what such actions could bring. He was acting as a young schoolboy, oblivious of the risks.

He removed a clove cigarette from his desk and lit it. As he puffed at the petite cigarette, he pulled out the gift that was wrapped in the black tissue paper. The note card smelled of Nicole's perfume.

He held the card to his nose and thought, "She must have sprayed it with the scent that she wears—the perfume I bought her."

Nico bought the same perfume for Piper so that when he was with her, he would think of his lover. Piper did not wear the perfume; the scent did not fit her personality. The floral scent overwhelmed her. He took his time opening the gift.

"A gift from my lover; what could it be?" he said to himself as his faced shined with pride.

He tore open the tissue paper, revealing a new, crisp, white chef's jacket with navy blue satin ribbon buttons. It was tailor made and beautifully woven of fine cotton. He admired the fabric as he grabbed the garment by the shoulders to shake it into place. As the jacket unfolded, he noticed that his name had also been embroidered in navy blue thread. He felt proud as he looked at the name.

The name read in cursive writing, "Marco."

He looked at it again as if he had not seen it clearly. At second glance, there was no mistaking the name. It was crystal clear: "Marco."

Nico was overwhelmed with confusion. He slumped back heavily in his chair. A sharp twinge of reality struck his consciousness.

"This jacket was meant for him. Nicole was, or is, sleeping with Marco. Fucking cunt," he said to himself with words that resonated into the air as he repeated loudly, "Fucking cunt!"

Nico had to sit for a moment and collect the myriad of insecure thoughts that were running rampant over his rational ones, causing him pangs of nausea.

"Nicole is mine. She is my muse," he said, as if she was an object. Neither she nor he had exchanged sentiments of love, but he never allowed his mind to accept any possible chance that she was not in love with him.

Nico was not in love with Nicole, but that did not matter to him. She made him feel alive. He never contemplated that he could ever be the victim of such a twist of fate. Nico was used to Piper's loyalty and took for granted that all of the females he encountered would share that sentiment of loyalty to him.

Nico had never been a jealous man. He had never needed to possess such a trait. The woman in his life was assiduous and obsequious to him. He did not feel any sense of insecurity in their relationship. It began to sink into his consciousness as the thought, "She is fucking my employee behind my back? Why?" The reality of this concept was degrading to him.

Nico sat for over 30 minutes attempting to gather his emotions and make sense of the unpredicted turn of events. As the 30 minutes turned to 31 and then 32, his mind raced.

"I have to work this out with Piper. At the end of day, she is consistent. She would never do this to me," he thought. As the stress overwhelmed him, he reached into his desk drawer and took out a prescription bottle that read "Adavant." He attempted to push down on the plastic cap to open the bottle. It did not open. He tried again, pushing harder. The bottle slipped on the metal surface of his desk.

"Putain de merde!" he screamed as he picked up the bottle and threw it across the room and it smashed against the wall, spilling the small white pills onto the floor.

He ignored the irony of the tantrum as his thoughts swung from Nicole to Piper, but always back to Nicole. He could not forget the new, fresh love that was Nicole: the excitement of the first kiss, touch, and the anticipation of the sex, the "Sirens call"

"I will not lose her. I can control this," he thought. "I will not lose her to my employee; I will win her back." He began to motivate himself. He gathered his final thoughts as he stood up from his chair, beaming with newfound resilience.

"First, I will purchase for her a ticket to France."

He began to fold the jacket. He placed it back into the bag. "I will not let her know that I know about the gift for Marco," he thought as he stuffed the jacket back into the bag with the note card.

"What the fuck does Marco know about women?" he asked himself as he picked up his phone and dialed the extension number of his assistant, Anne Marie.

"Hello, this is Anne Marie."

"Anne Marie, this is Nico. Please purchase a plane ticket for an employee to attend the event with me in France," Nico directed her.

"Who is attending, Nico?" Anne Marie asked in a professional manner, without personal interjection.

"Nicole Miller," Nico flatly replied.

Anne Marie had been Nico's personal assistant for ten years; thus, she was used to his indiscretions and knew better than to ask questions.

"Certainly, Chef," she replied obediently. "I will text your Blackberry once I have confirmation."

Nico hung up without saying goodbye. Anne Marie was accustomed to this type of closing. He stood up and drew three more drags from the cigarette before smashing it into the small dirty, fusty ashtray that was already over-littered with butts. He blew out the smoke as he stared into the air. He grabbed the bag and headed for the office door, stepping on the pills that cluttered the floor as he exited.

Nico walked down the hall and stopped at the schedule that hung on the wall to check for Nicole's arrival time. His finger slid down the paper that was clipped to the board. Once he found her name, he squinted to bring the text into focus. He turned and walked back into his office, which he had left unlocked. He entered the office and closed the door behind him. He reached back into his pocket and pulled out his desk keys. He sat at his chair and placed the small key into the desk drawer lock and turned it. He pulled at the drawer before realizing that he had left the drawer unlocked and had just locked it. He repeated the steps, unlocking the drawer this time.

He pulled the drawer open and reached his hand to the back, feeling the items. He stopped and pulled out a small white plastic bag of cocaine. He grabbed one of his business cards from the top of the cluttered desk and placed a small amount of the white powder onto the edge of the thick white business card. He bent over and snorted the powder. He repeated the act using his other nostril, placed the baggie in his pants, locked the desk drawer, and left the office, locking the door this time.

Nico reached the main kitchen and called out across the room, "Marco, come!"

Marco came quickly, as soon as he heard Chef's call for him.

"This is for you." Nico held out the gift bag. Marco looked confused. Nico spoke disconcertedly, "I grabbed it thinking it was from Piper; it seems it is not. It appears to be for you, from a lady admirer."

Marco laughed awkwardly. "Get out," he replied.

"It is for you, I am certain." Nico handed him the bag, walked away, grabbed a clean apron from the top shelf, and began to tie it around his chef's jacket. He looked down at the ground and then up to the bow he was tying around his waist.

Nico had engaged in several extemporaneous relationships over the years, but this one had the most potential for damage to his marriage. He was at an age and mental state where he depended on the visceral highs of the relationship. He felt a much needed rush of testosterone from their sex and a sense of euphoria when he was around her youth and vivacity. Though he continued to have sex with Piper, he had difficulty getting aroused. Piper knew there was something wrong. He dismissed her suspicion as merely common course of behavior for her temperament.

Before starting his terrine of the day, he reached into his pocket and pulled out his cell phone.

"Hello, I am only five minutes away," Piper said in self-defense as she answered the phone.

"I just called to say I love you, ma chérie," Nico replied.

"I love you too, Nico," Piper said, as she was caught unsuspecting of the sudden sentimental act.

"That is all. I will see you soon. Be safe," he said and hung up.

Piper hung up the phone and tried to figure out what Nico's motives were. She felt that common feeling of distrust.

CHAPTER SIX
PAIN IN SILENCE

Piper's hours, minutes, and seconds were measured. Her time was not valued by her standards but by others' expectations of her. Nico critiqued her during the time that made up any given 24 hours in a day, the 52 weeks in a year, or the 365 days that measured yet another calendar period. Piper felt the stress with every movement of the second hand of her Cartier watch with Nico's inscription engraved on the back: "I treasure every minute with you. Forever, Nico."

She glanced down at her left wrist as she exceeded the average speed on the freeway en route to the restaurant. As usual, she was late, however, not by her standards. If not for Piper's sports car, she would be more dilatory than her standard.

She reveled in the fact that she had the plane tickets for France booked. The seats were chosen and the frequent flyer miles assured. The hotel was reserving their favorite room. She did not have time to make bookings to champagne houses, but the hotel would make those plans upon arrival.

As she thought about the last-minute chores that were required of her, she sped through a yellow light and a stop sign until finally pulling into the back of the restaurant.

"Fifteen minutes late, as usual. Why am I always 15 minutes late? Why always 900 seconds? Wouldn't life be fantastic if I had a spare 900 seconds?" she thought to herself as she grabbed her large, yellow Hermes bag and bottle of Evian from the seat.

She slammed the door with her knee and pressed the lock, nestling the Evian bottle under her chin.

"Shit, my cell phone," she said aloud. The Evian bottle dropped and the keys fell to the asphalt. She looked up at the sky and laughed. "Okay, let's take a step back and a deep breath. My happy place, my happy place…" she thought.

After retrieving her phone, Piper gathered her composure as always and entered the back door of the restaurant. When the restaurant door slammed shut, space and time were breeched by the immediate noise of the kitchen breaking the seal of the outside world.

A kitchen has a life and energy of its own. The pace, mood, and personality of the head chef mediate and influence the tone of all personalities that work within its confines.

Nico was fast, selective, quiet, but overall, intimidating. Regardless of the individual personalities of the chefs, everyone working with Nico lost their individual personality while at work.

Piper caught a glimpse of Nico leaning over the counter, holding a chef's knife with grace and authority. His eyes were fixed on the raw meat that he was methodically deboning. The skill and grace of his movements were beautiful and fluid. Piper stopped a moment and stared at him in awe of his skill and talent.

"He looks so intense and inspiring," she thought to herself, "Just as the day we met."

She often saw Nico in this vein. She chose to remember this man as opposed to the person he became after the stress, pressure, and embeddings of their marriage tamed his spirit.

Nico did not look up, which was no surprise to Piper. She made a sharp left and entered the office. She placed her purse and personal items behind the desk and grabbed a jacket customized with her name on the left side. She buttoned the jacket and took a clean apron from the side chair. She left the room, tying the apron around the back and then at the front of her small waist.

She walked into the kitchen, this time, calling out to Nico. "Hello, hello!" she said cheerily and loudly. The other chefs smiled and looked up, returning the greeting. The staff was genuinely pleased to see Piper. The kitchen absorbed the warm, pleasant, positive aura she emitted.

Nico did not look up but said aloud, "Bonjour, ma chérie. A quelle heure? I thought you said 15 minutes. That was an hour ago, non?"

"It's time to give you a wet, sloppy kiss," she laughed as she kissed his cheek, displacing his attentions as he worked methodically.

"Piper, off with you," he replied with a slight smile.

She laughed as she walked to her pastry kitchen. There, she was greeted by her chefs.

"Hello, Chef," each one called out to her.

"Hello, my children," she replied warmly.

Piper's chefs were much younger than Nico and much closer to her age. She looked after them as if they were her flock. She became involved with their lives, strife, joys, and hardships. Piper knew them all personally.

"How is the chocolate cashew tart? Did the cashew brittle break up like we designed?" she asked Laurent as she opened the refrigerator door.

"Yes, it is most beautiful, Chef," replied Laurent.

Laurent was her sous chef. He was second in line and the most talented of her ducklings. This was a term she lovingly used to refer to them.

Piper looked at the tarts and the brittle that was firm and set in the long baking sheet.

"I am happy with it. I hope you are. I stayed late last night working on the sugar content," he said to her as he worked to the hum of the ice cream machine.

"Wow," she called out with joy. "Laurent, this is brilliant. They were sharing a moment of success.

However, the moment was invaded by a voice calling into the room asking for Piper. It was Nicole.

"Table 21 complained about the crème brulée last night, saying it was watery," the young girl spoke in a sharp, disrespectful tone. "More than one table complained, in fact."

Piper looked up at her disbelief at her tone. She walked back to the refrigerator and pulled out one of the prepared crème brulées. She placed it on the center island, grabbed a spoon, and stuck it into the mixture.

"This is perfectly set. Anyone can see that, Nicole." Piper snapped back at her.

Nicole did not respond. She picked up the ramekin, turned, and walked out.

Piper and her chefs looked at each other, laughed, and went back to work.

"Ten to one she is running as fast as her Payless shoes will carry her legs to Nico," Laurent said without a thought.

Piper looked at him, confused. "Why would she do that?"

"Hello," Laurent replied in a sarcastic tone.

"What, Laurent?" she asked. The other chefs scattered out of the room.

"Laurent, what are you talking about? Do you want to tell me what the hell is going on, as I am the only one who doesn't know?"

Laurent looked at her and spoke quietly. He had lost control of his words and realized that it was too late to retract them. "She is fucking Marco and told the entire kitchen and staff that she fucked Nico also."

Piper looked at him with wide, emoting eyes. She did not speak. Her eyes filled with water and she struggled to contain the tears within the confines of her large, defined, brown eyes.

"Does the entire restaurant know?" she asked as her voice broke up.

"I do not know, Chef," he replied in a sympathetic tone. I was just speaking aloud. I am sorry. I shouldn't have said anything." He walked away with his head lowered.

Piper stood frozen in place. She looked at her reflection in the stainless steel counter glaring back at her.

"All was obvious now to everyone but me," she said as she stared at her reflection, which mirrored her sorrow.

She began to recall the instances during the last week when she had seen Nicole with Nico. "I passed her walking out of Nico's office last week." She began to see things from a new perspective, with introspect. "I thought that was out of place. I felt it in my heart."

She recalled the awkward stare from Nico that pierced the silence when she walked in after having passed Nicole in the hallway. She felt sick and dizzy. She placed her hands on the countertop and braced her weight forward, off her feet.

One single tear fell from her eyes onto the sterile surface. She brushed it off with her hand and gathered her composure. She stood and turned, walking mercurially toward the main kitchen.

She pushed past the chefs who were in the way of her determined path.

"I knew it!" she spoke aloud softly, over and over again, with the rage inside her building each time she visualized Nico and this woman having sex. Piper felt uncontainable rage.

She walked into the main kitchen and found Nico prepping plates with Marco. Nicole was not in the kitchen.

"Nico, tell me about Nicole!" she shouted from a distance, rigid and tense. Marco and Nico stopped working immediately and looked up at her with surprise. Chefs rarely look up from plating a main course mid-stream.

Nicole entered the main kitchen without time to turn around and exit unnoticed.

"Don't go anywhere, Nicole," Piper yelled at her. "This involves you too." She turned back toward Nico, "Do you have something to tell me, Nico?" she screamed in a demanding voice none of the employees had heard before.

Nico looked at her and laughed, "You are off balance Piper. Calm down. You are making a fool of yourself, and me." He commented calmly initially, but emphasized the latter words with passion and annoyance. In reality, Nico was aware that she had not acted petty or overly emotional; he knew he had been caught and this was more disturbing to Nico than the chastising public display.

"Did Nicole come to tell you about table 21's discontent with my crème brulée?" she laughed sarcastically, "Or did she come to ask you to fuck her brains out after service?"

She smiled coldly with her arms folded over her chest and her head cocked to one side.

Nico walked over to her and grabbed her arm, tugging at her in an attempt to escort her out of the main kitchen toward their office.

"Oh, what, Nico, you think they don't all already know?" Piper yelled out, as she was dragged behind him. Nico did not speak to her; he merely ushered her uncomfortably and aggressively. He moved her quickly into the quiet confines of the office, out of the employees' curious, apathetic stares. He pushed her into the office and slammed the door behind them.

"Piper, have you lost your fucking mind?" he yelled.

"No, Nico, I have not lost my fucking mind, but it seems you have. Fucking the server? Really, is this what has become of you? And me, for that matter? Did I interrupt your little intimate session last week? Remember?" She was quick in an attempt to catch him off guard.

"No, I remember you walking into my office after Nicole left, after discussing her hours for this week," Nico replied with a callous calmness to his voice. His mind was calm, although his palms were beginning to sweat with the guilt over the obvious predicament. "You, my dear, need to calm down and realize what an ass you are making of yourself, and me, may I add." He laughed as he spoke in a demeaning, irreverent tone. He played a premeditated game now, one of intimidation, one of poker.

Piper walked over to the desk where he had sat down with legs crossed. This was one of Nico's tactical moves of dominance and control. She stood in place, staring, fixing her eyes on his. His pupils rapidly looked back and forth while he blinked several times a second.

"Nico, I know what is going on. The chefs in this kitchen know what is going on. If you do not tell me, I will go back into my little kitchen, as you put it, and grab the biggest knife I can find. I will then return and fucking cut your petite balls away from your dick just as meticulously as you cut up your fucking duck breasts. Now, once more, do you want to tell me what is going on with you and Nicole?" She screamed at him this time as she began to lose her composure. The muscles in her neck strained as she tried to keep herself from crying. She knew that would reduce her validity to a hormonal bitch in his eyes.

Nico realized that this was more than a mere woman's jealous intuition. He realized that he could have truly damaged his marriage. His frivolity could have caused permanent devastation in his life and his business. He just looked at her, incapable of commenting.

Piper stopped at the very moment Nico fell silent.

"This is not my life. This is not happening," she thought to herself. "He fucked her," she admitted it to herself. "His eyes speak volumes; they give him up."

Nico did not need to admit, deny, or weave an intricate denial tale. Both of them sadly realized that neither of them would ever be the same. Regardless of what he had done, she was aware that he was not hers anymore. The special sacred closeness that she felt she shared with her husband was gone. Another woman had entered that sanctum. Although she felt in her heart that he was no longer hers, she refused to believe it.

She wanted to scream, throw the nearest object, and pummel Nico's face with her fists. She looked down at the desk and saw the brass pig paperweight that she bought him the year they opened the restaurant. She envisioned picking it up and throwing it at his head. She could vividly see her performing this action in her mind, but she could not act it out; it was within her mind, but could not be released. She merely looked at him, attempting to communicate her pain and sorrow through her eyes, through the tears that now flowed from her eyes.

Piper often condemned herself for lacking the strength and conviction to act out her inner thoughts, whether sorrow or anger. Others would say that she had a quiet, collective calmness. Piper saw the caged in emotions as a weakness of character. Most mistook her redolence for acceptance. What they could not see was that inside of Piper was a tumultuous wave of emotion churning and ebbing with abated patience for Nico's indiscretions.

Nico stood up and she reacted. Her mind told her to flee. As he stood, his chair rolled in the opposite direction; she reached down and grabbed her purse once his chair obstructed his direct path to her. Nico didn't try to stop her. Piper turned and ran out the door. She ran down the hall trying to keep a respectful hold on her emotions. She did not make eye contact with anyone, except Marco. He was in the main kitchen, looking out into the hall with a bewildered look on this face. He did not speak to her. The look on his face was one of hurt. His mind was also trying to piece together the fragments of the relationships that had collided.

She pushed the door open, and the chilled morning air slapped her in the face, as her cheeks were now wet from her tears. She reached into her purse and lost her grip on it, dropping it on the ground instead.

"Ahhhh!" she yelled as she bent down to pick up the contents that had spilled out. She picked up the keys and unlocked her car, running the last few steps to gain access to the quiet cavity. She backed out of the parking lot without looking back. She knew Nico would not run after her. She was not accustomed to such chivalrous moves from him. That was not his style, especially when he was guilty.

Piper reached over and inside her purse. She felt around until her fingers located her pill case. She opened the small enameled and embellished case that Nico had bought her in Italy and removed a small oval pill; she knew it was the sedative by touch. She placed the pill onto her dry tongue and let out a sigh while simultaneously shaking her head in disbelief. She drove, trying to escape her pain. The vision of Nico and Nicole replayed in her mind. His lack of response resonated within her heart. She sped down the freeway toward her home.

She brushed her tears away with the back of her hand as she nervously looked in the rear view mirror. She noticed a red and white flashing light behind her car.

"Shit, I am being pulled over?" she said aloud. She immediately pulled off the freeway and onto the slip road. She could not suffer the ramifications of a public arrest. She took a deep breath and hit the button to retract the window. As the State Trooper walked toward her open window, she glanced out at him, not sure if she wanted to cry for help or act as if nothing was wrong.

"Ma'am, I need to see your license and registration card," he said stoically.

"Why? Was I speeding?" she replied, knowing that she was.

He took a step forward and leaned over closer to her face. She recoiled. She tried to look away, hoping her bloodshot eyes were not swollen from the tears. He did not speak nor move. She could not see his eyes. She could only see her own in his dark mirrored sunglasses. To avoid suspicion, she had no choice but to look directly at him.

"Are you alright, ma'am?" he asked as though he could see right through her façade. Piper thought she had done an adequate job of concealing her sorrow. She looked at him quietly, without speaking. She did not know if she would burst into tears. She tried not to move a single facial muscle. She looked directly into his eyes. Her eyes screamed of her sorrow like a crowded stadium. There was no silence; there was nothing quiet about the pain within her eyes.

"Please remove me; please rescue me from this life," she thought, her words screaming inside her mind.

The trooper stood still for a moment, looking at her. The silence continued for seconds, but they seemed like hours.

"Ma'am, are you alright?" he repeated.

Piper realized at that moment that he was not reading her eyes. He was not seeing her pain. She looked away and reached into her purse for the perfunctory and rudimentary information. She pulled out her license and registration card. She did not look into his eyes again. Once again on this night, she felt betrayed in a sense. The trooper handed her a ticket and told her in very plain words, "Slow down and have good night, ma'am."

She pulled back onto the road, defused from the rush of anger she was feeling when she left Petite Piper, but more despondent and alone. She arrived at their home, pulled into the garage, and put the car in park. She sat for a moment in the dark garage. Her fast, beautiful, expensive car could not flee the impending night that she was acutely and painfully aware would be difficult.

Once inside, she opened a bottle of wine and carried it into her bedroom. She closed the door and wondered whether Nico would come home.

"Will he go to her house? He couldn't do that to me. Would he?" She drank after each thought. "In ten hours, my entire life has changed." She felt suddenly ill and made it to her bathroom just before vomiting into her toilet. She lay on the marble floor of the master bathroom crying and clutching the stone cold marble, attempting to find some comfort that would not come from her surroundings, Nico, or from within.

CHAPTER SEVEN
PRETENDING

The next day found Nico at 5:30 A.M., hung over, on the couch, and waking to an aching back and pounding head. By the time he had arrived home from the restaurant, Piper was asleep with the bedroom door locked. He did not wake her, in part, due to his lack of conviction and strength. Nico felt that in his experience with Piper, it was best to let her be. He did not have the communication nor relationship skills to speak to her effectively. If he opened the door to communication with her, he did not have the patience to see it through to a productive resolution.

He opened his eyes and sat up for a moment before deciding what his actions would be. He did not shower or change. Nico always had a change of clothes and a shaving kit at the restaurant in case of such an emergency. He did not stop once he stood up. He walked straight through the house to the garage and got into his car. He glanced at Piper's car, noticing that it was parked crooked. He had not noticed it when he got in the night before.

"She must have been upset when she drove into the garage." He glanced into the car and saw that her purse was still on the front seat. He spotted the yellow speeding ticket beside the purse. "I am glad I did not take her on last night," he thought, failing to grasp the magnitude of the situation.

As he pulled away from their home, he looked up at the window that looked into Piper's bedroom. In his arrogant haste, he did not reflect on his actions and how they may have devastated Piper. He did not allow his mind to wander past his own consumed thoughts of himself. He looked back at the road ahead and thought, "By this afternoon, she will have gotten it out of her system. She has no proof. Deny, deny, deny, Nico; it has always served you well."

As the distance between Nico and Piper grew larger, Piper awoke, not to her alarm clock but to the prodding of the sun. She opened her eyes and looked over at Nico's side of the bed. No signs of Nico; no signs that he had slept with her. She felt empty inside.

"Maybe this did not happen. Maybe I dreamt it last night," she thought as she lay there recounting the events. Once again, she was feeling extreme nausea come in waves. "What is going on?" she thought as she sat up and felt her head to see if she was feverish.

Nico was not there. She was alone. Her life felt disjointed and lost. She felt uneasy and short of breath. She thought about Nico, Nicole, and the State Trooper. She wished it had all been a dream, but she knew it was not.

The waves of nausea swelled. She leapt out of bed just in time to make it to the bathroom. Just making it to the toilet, she lifted the lid and grabbed the rim of the bowl. She threw up as every tired muscle in her arms grabbed the bowl for leverage.

Piper had an idea of what was wrong with her. Her period was three weeks late. She lifted her weary head and placed it in her hands.

She looked up at the medicine cabinet. She had purchased a pregnancy test, but was delaying taking it. She was not ready to know the truth.

Being pregnant would anger Nico tremendously. He did not want any interference with his life or his success. Piper, however, would be disappointed if the test was negative. She would love to have children.

Once she felt well enough to stand up, she grabbed a washcloth and placed it in the sink. As the cold water filled the sink, she looked into the mirror. She touched her eyes, swollen and red, then her nose, red and sore.

"Get a grip, Piper," she said to herself as she ran her fingers through her hair. "I have to take this test," she said as she reached up and opened the mirrored door. She removed the box containing the test and turned the water off. She walked over to the toilet and sat down to take the test.

She held it underneath her body and then brought it up to her line of vision. She took in a deep breath as she starred at the stick.

"Okay," she said as she walked over to the shower and reached in to turn on the water. After condensation formed on the glass, she opened the door, stepped in, and allowed the warm water to run over her face. She hoped to wash away the sickness, pain, and reality. Piper was pregnant.

She stood in the shower for 30 minutes or more, allowing herself the necessary time to accept the facts and attempt rejuvenation. Upon terminating the purification of the shower, she realized that she was late, once again. She recalled that there was a private booking tonight.

"Shit, I have to call Laurent. I didn't make the petite fours and dark chocolate soufflés."

She stopped again as she caught her image in the steamy mirror. There, in quiet solitude, she stood gazing into the mirror. She asked herself, "Will you let this happen to your life, to your marriage, and now, your soon-to-be-child? This is a fling with a money grubbing, young waitress. Get it together." She sighed. "Disappointment? Abandonment? Loneliness? This is not my destiny." Tears filled up her swollen eyes. She wiped away the condensation from the foggy mirror.

She grabbed a towel and held it to her eyes. "I cannot do this. I will not do this. I cannot lose this marriage. What am I doing wrong?" she asked herself.

"Enough, Piper! I am bigger than this," she said aloud as she started to mentally compose herself. She walked out of the bathroom and into her bedroom. "I need to make some tea, try and eat some toast, and get my ass to the restaurant before all this shit hits the fan."

As she walked to the kitchen, she noticed a small piece of paper by the couch. She bent down and picked it up. It was notes from Anne Marie, Nico's personal assistant. It was Nico's flight and hotel itinerary for his upcoming trip to France. He was going on a celebrity chef junket in Northern France. It had been arranged that she would stay behind to manage the restaurant.

"I will meet him in France," she thought with renewed hope for their future. "France is our magical place." She reached for the phone to call Anne Marie, but stopped herself. "Forget that. I'll just pack and go to the airport. I'll call Laurent on my way." She was excited, positive, and convinced. A warm sense of optimism overwhelmed her.

"This is it; I am going to surprise Nico in France. Screw all of this. I can make this right. I can make him love me again," she said with no doubt in her mind.

CHAPTER EIGHT
THE WHELPING

Jacquemart's days were blending together. The days were blending into nights and the nights seemed never ending. He grew irritable and impatient. He was lonely, but despised companionship, unless, of course, it was his ever loving loyal CeCeine. He was not sure of the time, but he saw the sun beginning to set over the far end of the estate. With a bottle of cognac in hand, he sat up from the small cot he occupied in the small shed outside the walls of the sprawling abandoned and dilapidated estate. He stood up and looked out the window at the château. He did not see it for what it was: ruins. He saw it as it appeared when he was a very small boy, running down the halls, hiding in the closets of the many rooms, running and playing on the vast grounds and ornate gardens.

He looked through the window of the turret that stood as it did when he was a child. It still housed the faded curtains and now warped furniture from rain falling through the missing slate tiles. There, in the hall, he saw his stepmother as she walked past the window. Suddenly, she stopped and turned back around toward the window, sporting a sapphire blue organza dress, her hair tied back, and her black eyes fixed out the window at him.

"HIDE! Don't let her see me," he said to himself as he stooped down, heart pounding, face in hands, covering his eyes. "Shhh, don't speak; don't breathe." He sucked in the air around him and held it deep within his lungs. "See if she's gone," he said as he slowly inched up off the ground. He placed his free hand on the windowsill and peered over the edge.

"She's gone," he said as he sat back down and breathed out the air that he was holding in. He brought the bottle to his lips and titled it, allowing the amber liquor to flow past his lips and into his mouth, burning each piece of dry skin that it touched.

"Tonight, I will sneak out of the shed and find a date." He had done this many times as a teenager. He was not allowed to bring friends of any form to the château. He would entertain classmates, and infrequently, women, in this very same timber shed. His male classmates merely came to have a look for themselves at the château that had become folklore and historical in the small town. There were rumors of the family and of Jacquemart's mom trying to drown him at birth. The story of his stepmother drinking on Friday nights at the local bar while his father was working and he was locked in his bedroom was one of the many infamous, colorful stories that circulated amongst the townspeople.

Jacquemart stood up and wiped his lips with the back of his hand. He set the cognac down on the table and tucked his shirt into his dirty, baggy pants. He ran his fingers through his thick, long hair and opened the door of the small barren room. He stepped into his truck and started down the winding road to the entrance of his prison. As he drove through the gate that remained opened, he did not feel a sense of freedom. He lived in a constant state of stress and urgency. He checked his watch minute by minute although he had no commitments to keep.

"She will find out that I've left my room if I'm gone too long," he thought to himself as his mind turned back to the delusional figure that walked the halls continually tormenting and taunting him, his stepmother. He was ten years old, living in the château.

"You are a cocotte's (whore's) bastard; worthless and wasted." He heard the voice resonate over and over again.

His anxious thoughts turned toward a release.

"They're all whores. They bring us into this world through fucking, getting a dick in their cunts. I am not one of those cunts." All he could think of was his displaced anger. The rage replayed redundantly in his mind like and addiction.

One sip of cognac turned into gulps. Gulps turned into the blurred movement of all figures surrounding him. It was not long before he dropped the empty bottle and lay on the floor, passed out.

Jacquemart awoke to the sound of moaning and yelping. He sat up and strained to hear the sound, to bring it into recognizable sounds. "CeCeine."

He leapt to his feet and ran down the hall toward the kitchen. In the small hall beside the kitchen was a coatroom. There, CeCeine lay on the floor, laboring, whining, and laboring. She was giving birth. Jacquemart birthed her every year to various pure bloodhounds to keep his pack strong and healthy.

At the sight of her, his heart sunk and his stomach twisted. He had never neglected her during her time of need. She had birthed three pups that lay beside her, eyes closed, bloody, but breathing, struggling and squirming to feel the heat of their mother.

The pup she was birthing had descended and was lying just outside of her body. She was biting at the young pup, the blood not yet removed from its body. Jacquemart ran over and knelt down on the bloodied floor beside her and the newly birthed pup. As he pushed the mucus and blood aside, he could not see the head of the pup. CeCeine continuously bit and licked at the young pup.

"CeCeine, non," he yelled at her as he tried to work through the shocking scene that had woken him from his drunken slumber. He picked the young pup up and placed his ear to its small motionless mouth. He could not see its chest moving or mouth open to indicate signs of life. He pried the small mouth open and breathed into it, giving it air to fill its new lungs.

He did not see a reaction. The pup's umbilical cord had been gnawed through. The pup lay motionless in his hands. Its death was at his hands.

CeCeine had birthed five pups and was tired and labored. Jacquemart did not see it this way. He saw a young life struggling and dying at the hands of a mother who carelessly birthed it and then abandoned it.

Rage and retribution filled his body and mind. As CeCeine lay motionless, he kicked her. "Fuck you, you worthless cocotte!" he screamed as he stood up with the young pup still in his hands. Blood still covered his lips, providing evidence of his failed attempts. He walked the pup over to the kitchen. He reached down and opened one of the drawers with his hand, smearing blood on the drawer. He removed a towel and wrapped it around the dead pup. He lifted the small, lifeless body to his lips and kissed it as tears filled his eyes.

He set the swaddled body down on the table and turned back to the set of drawers in the large kitchen. He slowly opened the second drawer and removed a large carving knife.

He turned and walked slowly over to CeCeine, tears blurring his vision. He knelt down as she panted heavily, her young pups struggling to find the tit and warmth of their mother.

He did not hesitate before plunging the long, sharp blade into the throat of his loved, cherished companion.

"Fucking bitch. You birthed life. Fucking worthless cunt, it is not at your hands. Once you gave birth, they had a right to live a life. Murderer."

He sobbed as he screamed and slurred the words. The knife ripped down her chest to her stomach, spilling her organs onto the antique marble floor that had seen a history of sorrow.

Blood spilled and covered CeCeine's lifeless body. Jacquemart's pants were now covered in her blood. The color of her fur was unrecognizable as the thick, dark fluid saturated it.

He dropped the knife and grabbed her by the hind legs, dragging her body toward the preparation room. A long trail of blood followed from her body, exposing the trail of those murderous last minutes. Her pups were still squirming and crying out for their mother.

Once CeCeine was in the preparation room, Jacquemart grabbed her two front legs and then her two back legs and lifted her into the sink, hog-tied. Her intestines spilled out to the floor. Blood flowed as her head jerked back with a lifeless glaze from the once emotional eyes. She was no longer recognizable to him. This was not the loyal life companion. He had lost all sense of reason and logic. CeCeine was now the symbol of loathing that represented his mother.

Jacquemart let out a loud yell as he began to fillet her as coldly as if she was a boar, stag, or hare. His arms, hands, and finger nails were covered with the stains of her life.

Once he had the meat from her body, he opened the cabinet under the sink and pulled out the garbage can. He picked her up for the last time and dropped her into the garbage can. He dragged the can through the room and outside to the hog shed. The sound of a human stirred the animals to movement, conditionally snorting and scratching their hooves on the ground. Jacquemart recognized that this meant it was feeding time. He lifted the garbage can over the fence and dumped CeCeine's body onto the ground. The hogs ripped into her body and bit through her bones and into her meat. They circled around the body, devouring her remains. Jacquemart dragged the garbage can back toward the house. He arrived at the door and turned on the hose to swill out the bloodied garbage can. He acted as he had done a thousand times feeding the hogs meat. Once the can was clean, he turned it upside down and walked through the door, leaving the door handle covered in CeCeine's blood.

As he entered the house, the sound of the pups yelping stirred him to the present. He walked over them as they stretched out their young bodies, yearning for the warmth of their mother. By this time, there were no remains of her.

Jacquemart casually walked over to them. He lifted his leg and slammed his boot downward onto a fragile, soft skull. The bones underneath the force of his boot crunched and buckled. Blood and brain matter squirted onto his pant leg and the floor. He stopped and turned to the next puppy and did the same. This time, he was quicker and more forceful, and with the next, even more so. By the time he reached the last puppy, he was stomping down with an uncontrollable force.

Within moments, the sound of life ceased. The movement stopped. All that remained was a blood-filled room with fragments of the young animals. Jacquemart turned away once more and walked through the halls of the mansion, up the stairs, and to his small cell. He sat on the bed and placed his head in his hands momentarily to rake his fingers through his dark, damp hair. He looked at the wall in front of him. He was conflicted. He already felt the loss of his love, CeCeine. He already felt the guilt from his impassioned actions. He did not know why or how he had become so robotic in his actions. He stopped being a man, and for that moment, was a living figure of his painful past acting out his pain and anger. A split second before gutting CeCeine, he thought that the pain would be released with her blood and heart. It was not. He felt more lonely, despondent, and confused than ever.

"Why didn't the whore succeed in killing me at birth? Those puppies were the lucky ones. I saved their souls." He lifted his legs onto the bed and lay flat, staring at the ceiling until his eyelids closed out the reality of the night's events.

CHAPTER NINE
FALLING APART

"The captain has turned on the seatbelt sign. Please return to your seats and secure your seatbelts."

Piper did not move. She stared at the stick with the blue plus sign marked clearly in the circle. She looked into the mirror in disbelief at her reflection.

"This is the second test. I am definitely pregnant," she said to herself. Just then, the plane jerked her forward, causing her to drop the pregnancy test into the sink that was filled with water left over from other passengers who had washed their hands.

"Shit!" She reached into the soapy water to retrieve it. "Oh, damn it," she said as she lifted the stick out using only her forefinger and thumb. She moved it over to the trash can lid and pushed it open, disposing of the dripping stick.

A knock at the door caused her to jump. "Ma'am, please return to your seat," a woman's voice called out to her.

Piper opened the door and made her way down the aisle, reaching for each seat back to brace her against the turbulent air pushing the plane around freely.

She sat in her seat, put her head back, and closed her eyes as she thought to herself, "What am I am going to tell Nico? He is going to be so upset."

Piper and Nico had talked about children, and Nico had made it clear that he was not inclined to dedicate his life to raising a child and abandon his career. Piper had been taking birth control until recently, when she felt it was no longer needed, based on the amount of sex that they were having, or in their case, not having.

Before she realized it, the plane had landed. She walked through the airport, pushing past strangers, talking, laughing, and holding babies. The emotional deluge of the positive test, the last-minute international trip, and Nico's latest fling was burdening her. She rented a car and drove to the hotel without much time spent in the moment. Her mind was tired and unable to focus as she drove.

"Once I get to the hotel and check in, I will lie down, shower, and take a walk. Nico will arrive in the morning, and I can play it by ear. I want this trip to save our marriage. I want this trip to save me," she thought as she pulled into the parking lot of the country manner turned private hotel.

"Bonjour, Madame, may I help you?" asked the deskman. Piper did not respond. Her eyes remained fixated her distorted appearance in the polished marble counter.

"Excusez-moi, madame, may I help you?" repeated the young Frenchman.

"Yes, I'm sorry. It was a long flight, and I am not paying attention. Yes, my name is Mrs. Blanche. The room is booked under my husband's name, Nico," replied Piper, attempting to appear pleasant and upbeat.

"Yes, Mrs. Blanche, I have the reservation right here. We welcome you and your husband back," he said, looking up from the computer and smiling at her.

Piper thought the comment strange. "This hotel keeps records a long time," she said to herself as she tried to recollect the last time she had stayed there.

"We have arranged to have you and your husband stay in the same room, as requested. Do you have luggage?" he asked.

"Yes, the bellman already has it. Thank you." She reached out and picked up the key that had a champagne cork as a keychain attached to it. She collected her purse and placed her wallet back inside it. She turned and followed the bellman who was standing off to the side with her bags.

"How was your trip, madame?" the older man with small round wire glasses asked.

"It was fine, thank you." Piper was not interested in making casual conversation at this point. All she could think of was the soft bed with crisp white hotel sheeting awaiting her.

They walked through the courtyard, down pea gravel walks, and to a small limestone stable block. The man stopped when he reached a large, brown, wooden stable door that had been converted into a large French door with two large wooden slat chairs and a bistro table.

"Here we are, Madame. May I have your key?" He turned and looked at her. He was short of breath and so was Piper. She held out the champagne cork for him.

As the two entered the room, Piper was determined to make any conversation short and to the point.

"Please have a bottle of champagne brought to the room, café au lait, croissants, and a fromage plate," she asked as she sat on the bed and slipped off her shoes. She had not eaten on the plane, but at that moment, she was not nauseous. She assumed that her body had been fooled into thinking it was much later than it was at that moment in France.

"Certainly, madame," the courteous bellman replied.

As soon as the door clicked shut, Piper tore off her clothes, went into the bathroom, grabbed a hotel robe, and laid back.

The phone rang, waking her from her sleep. She picked it up, finding it difficult to focus on her watch.

"Mrs. Blanche, this is the manager at the front of the house. Can you please meet me at the front desk?" asked a man with a heavy French accent.

Piper sensed something was aberrant, "Is there a problem?" she asked.

"Yes, there is a rather uncomfortable situation here," he responded.

"Alright, I will be there in a few minutes," she said as she thought, "Rather uncomfortable situation? What the hell does that mean?"

She dressed quickly and started to turn the large, black metal French door handle when the phone rang again.

"What is going on?" Piper responded with agitation.

"Madame, this is the manager again, Please bring your passport," he requested.

"My passport? For what?" Her pitch was high and her voice, loud.

He did not answer; he merely hung up the phone.

"Ah, the French can be so rude," she said aloud as she grabbed her purse and slammed the door shut behind her.

As she entered the front of the old manor, the manager appeared through a private office in the back. He placed his hand on her shoulder and moved her back out the door. "We seem to have a delicate matter here. May I see your identification please?" He spoke to her in a very soft, quiet voice.

Piper did not return the quiet composure. "Why, what is going on? Is it my husband? Is everything alright?" A wave of nausea overtook her body and she held her hand to her stomach. The thought of Nico being injured or dead was overwhelming.

"Are you alright, madame? Can I get you some water?" the manager asked with little empathy in his voice as he looked at her.

"No, you can tell me what the hell is going on. Can I go in and sit down please?" Piper contained her composure and pushed past him, attempting to open the door to the front desk.

"Madame, I would prefer it if you stayed out here until we resolve this so as to not upset the other guests." He reached ahead of her and placed his hand on the door. "I must insist that I see your passport." His voice was firm and commanding, his tone matching hers.

Piper pressed her lips together trying to stop herself from verbally escalating the matter. She allowed one of the handles of her purse to fall forward and she lifted her knee up to brace the large bag, she rifled through the contents until she found her leather passport holder. She lifted it out and slapped it onto the manager's chest.

"Here. Here is my passport. Now, tell me what is going on before I check out," she shouted at the man.

He did not answer her. He opened the wallet and removed her passport. He held it up to the light and said, "Follow me, madame."

Piper marched behind the manager back into the lobby and stopped just short of his office. He pointed to the chair in his office. A woman with her back facing the door was sitting in the chair. He put his hand down and leaned in to speak very softly again. "Mrs. Blanche, this woman has just checked in using your name. Can you identify her?"

"No, not unless I see her face," Piper sharply replied. "This is crazy, call the police." Piper once again pushed past the manager and walked into the room. "Who the hell do you think you are?" she screamed out to the woman.

The blonde-haired woman stood up, turned, and looked directly at Piper.

The air from Piper's lungs collapsed and her stomach revolted from the shock. Piper leaned over and threw up, catching it with her hand.

The manager turned and shouted for the bellman, "Get some towels, and water, Gerald, quickly."

"That is really melodramatic, Piper," Nicole said.

Piper stood up tall after a second and replied, "What are you doing here? Is Nico okay?" She was still thinking that something had gone grossly wrong and Nicole was sent to summon her back to the States.

"Piper, Nico flew me here, to be with him." She portentously smiled as she spoke.

The manager was handed a towel by the bellman. He reached in and handed it to Piper as he walked in and closed the door.

"Maybe you two would like to have some time to discuss the matter. I must remind you that I have other guests in the lobby." He ushered Nicole to sit back down. He appeared very nervous as he fervently attempted to assuage the matter.

"I am not staying. Nicole, tell Nico I hope you two are very happy. Tell him not to call me and not to return to our home until I move out. Oh, and you, you pathetic little money grubbing whore, you are beneath me." Piper turned and opened the door; she walked out without closing it, past the front desk and out the front door.

As her feet pounded the gravel walkway, the sound seemed miles away. She could no longer see from the tears that welled up in her eyes but had not yet fallen. She did not reach up to brush them away. She kept walking back to the room.

When she arrived, she opened the door and the room tray with the champagne had arrived. A bouquet of white lilies sat on the round country table. Lilies were Piper's favorite flowers. Nico always had an arrangement sent to their room when they traveled. Tears were now consistently flowing down her cheeks. She walked over to it, removed the card, and opened it. The card read, "Let me introduce you to my homeland. Let's experience the love, passion, and food of France, my little fraise."

Piper looked at the flowers and gasped for air. She could not breathe. She was filled with so much pain; she felt an agony of endless dimensions. She felt as if someone had amputated her right arm. The loss of Nico was infinite. He was her husband, best friend, business partner, cooking coach, and companion.

She walked over to the door and locked it. She picked up the phone and called the front desk. When the phone was answered, she asked for the manager.

"This is the manager, Mrs. Blanche. How may we help you with this difficult situation? Would you like me to find you another hotel?" He appeared more empathetic than before.

"No, that will not be necessary. I am going to return to the States. Can you please assure me, however, that I will have some time to gather my composure? When I leave the hotel, I will call you. Please, do not allow that woman to come to this room until I leave." She forced back the tears as she spoke. By the last sentence, she had started crying. "Thank you, that is all," she said and hung up.

Piper hung up the phone and fell onto the floor. She held her stomach and cried uncontrollably. She did not know how many minutes she had lost consumed with grief. She sat up, walked over to the desk, and sat down. She removed the hotel stationery and picked up a pen.

Dear Nico,

The sudden loss of you does not immediately pain me, for I am numb. Voices are ingratiating and comfort is shallow. Should I feel thankful or violated that rarely in life we find someone that we fall in love with secondly to friendship? Pain is now at the surface of my existence and I cannot imagine how I will ever experience another emotion."

Piper Blanche

When she signed her name, she set the pen down and placed the letter in an envelope, sealed it, and slipped the letter in her purse. She picked up the bottle of champagne for comfort, her suitcase that had not been unpacked, and opened the door. She did not stop to look back or contemplate her next steps. She did not call the front desk to tell them she was leaving. As she walked out the door and to the rental car, she tried to rally her spirits somehow.

"I came here for a new start, and this is an ending." Piper began to gasp for breath as she sobbed, "Oh God, what am I going to do?" She looked down at her stomach and placed her hand on it. "What is going to happen to us now?"

She picked up her suitcase and leaned over to her left side to balance the heavy bag. She dragged the bag outside the room and down the gravel path, stopping several times out of muscle exhaustion. She returned to the room and picked up her purse.

"I am going to send this letter to the States so Nico receives it when he returns," she removed the letter from her purse and wrote the restaurant address on the letter.

She grabbed the bottle of champagne and walked toward the door. She stopped as she grabbed the handle and walked out the door to her car. She stopped at the office and handed the letter to an employee at the desk, "Please mail this tomorrow, and bill the postage to the room."

She walked out and to the rental car. She started the car and stopped only to open the bottle of champagne. She drove without looking back, drinking from the bottle, continuous tears flowing from her eyes.

Lack of sleep, food, and mental respite were sprinting after Piper. She felt the effect of the bottle of champagne as she drove through the countryside, not entirely sure of where she was driving to. The controllable urge to urinate became uncontrollable. She could see ahead, off to the right, there was a pull off. Several trucks and a car were pulled off to the side. She could see a few women standing in a group talking.

"It must be a park." She pulled off to the side of the road behind the trucks. "At least I will be safe here. They must have a bathroom."

Piper stepped out of the car and walked away without locking it. She was light-headed and feeling drunk. Three women standing in a group stopped talking as she walked over to them.

"Excuse me, are there restrooms here?" she asked a young dark skinned woman. She was wearing a short sequence mini skirt and a black tank top, and high-heeled black boots. She did not answer Piper; she looked at her and shook her head as if she did not speak English. Piper asked the second woman in the group, "Parlez-vous anglais?" She received the same response.

Piper walked away annoyed and bereft. "There has to be a bathroom here," she mumbled as she stumbled through the woods.

A restroom did not appear. She began to walk down a hill, farther into the woods. She stopped by a large tree. "Fuck this; I have to go to the bathroom. I'll just go here; no one is around."

She squatted down and pulled down her pants. As she squatted to the ground, she lost her balance and fell over to her side. She could not get up. Face down into the dirt and leaves, the light around her turned black. She saw Nico's face, Laurent's face, and then nothingness. She had passed out.

Chapter 10
A Deeper Twist of Fate

The loss of his companion was wearing heavily on Jacquemart's psyche. The only companion he had known his entire thirty odd years of living was gone, and by his hand.

Wrought with confliction, Jacquemart did not know what he longed for more, CeCeine or the rush of adrenaline and the feeling of omniscient power that he had experienced while he was killing her. As he replayed the violent stabbing in his mind, he became aroused, and his penis grew harder with the image of each stabbing thrust into her womb.

His demented sexual release was interrupted by the sound of a car on the gravel drive. He did not allow nor invite anyone to the château. He jerked his hand out of his pants and zipped them up. He looked out the window at the car that had stopped on the drive. It was a black Range Rover. He was rankled by the intrusion. He stomped out of the kennels, gravel colliding with each heavy step, and toward the parked car.

Four men were in the car. As Jacquemart approached, the driver stuck his head out of the window and yelled out to him, "Where have you been, man? We are all waiting." The man spoke in a condescending British accent.

Jacquemart had lost all sense of time and commitment within the last 48 hours. He was living in a violent, enraged fantasy world fueled by the birth of the pups, CeCeine's actions toward her pup, and his birth mother. He had no compunction of conscience, only hatred toward females that he felt was justified by his abandonment at birth.

"Get your head back into your car before I tear it off and stuff it up your pasty white ass! Go!" Jacquemart screamed as the blood vessels in his temples surged, face red with anger, spitting as he screamed the words.

"What the bloody hell is wrong with you, you bastard frog?" the man replied in shock at Jacquemart's unpredicted aggression.

Jacquemart heard one word, bastard.

"You are the son of a cocotte, a jailed whore, you are a mistake, boy!" Jacquemart heard his stepmother laughing as she taunted him.

He ran toward the car in a great sprint. The Englishman, sensing the volatility of his actions, put up the window and placed the car in reverse. As he backed up, Jacquemart reached the car. He grabbed the door handle, but was seconds too late. He missed and stumbled to the ground, catching himself with his hands, stones pressing into his palms, cutting into his skin.

He stood up and yelled at the car as it reversed down his driveway, "I'll fucking kill you! I'm gonna fucking kill you!" He ran after the car down the drive. Realizing that he would not catch the vehicle, Jacquemart thought mercurially, "I know these grounds; he doesn't. I will cut through parcel number 25 and head this fuck off as he enters the highway."

Jacquemart ran through the woods with a paced speed, his breathing consistent, arms thrusting forward, and legs sprinting at a rate that would guarantee his ability to cut the car off as his property met the main highway.

As he panted to the rhythm of his strides, he could see only one vision ahead: his mother. Since he was a small boy, he had visualized the night he was born. As he imagined his mother attempting to drown him, he gasped for air.

"There, just ahead, the clearing. I see the road. This fucker is dead," he said as he broke stride and sprinted ahead.

As he reached the road, he stopped once in the middle of the two-lane highway. He looked to the left as he heard a car passing just as he stepped onto the asphalt. A black Range Rover was speeding off into the distance.

Jacquemart let out a scream that startled the birds from the trees. It echoed through the woods, stirring all that hid within the tree-lined buffer. He placed his palms onto his temples and squeezed his eyes shut as he turned around.

When he opened his eyes, he saw the vision of a woman through the trees. He stopped and walked over to the edge of the woods. He squatted down to avoid being seen. A woman off in the distance was on her knees bobbing her head. The vision of a second person came into focus, a man.

"Maman? Mother?" he asked in a state of dazed confusion. He sat quietly, watching the woman in the woods performing oral sex on the man, fueling his rage and igniting violent thoughts within his mind, playing out cutting, stabbing, and severing the whore's head from her body.

Common in many European woods is an area of ungoverned land, off heavy trucking routes, where pimps will drop off young prostitutes to stand in the woods waiting for truckers to pull off the road for sex, most commonly, oral sex. On this day, five young women of varying ages and races stood in the drizzling cold rain, smoking cigarettes and waiting for a patron.

Jacquemart watched until the service was complete. He observed as the woman stood up and wiped her mouth. The man zipped up his trousers and walked away. Jacquemart stood up and followed several paces behind the woman as she walked the path through the woods.

She stopped and looked behind her. Jacquemart stood behind a tree, back to the tree, staring ahead, holding his breath, hoping not to be discovered.

"If I can rid this world of just one whore, I can save a life. I could have never been born if someone had cared enough about man to do this to the whore who birthed me," he thought as he plotted to improve the state of the world, one whore at a time.

By the time he turned around, he lost sight of the woman. He searched to his left, and then right, but there was no sign of her. Annoyed and in disbelief that she could have evaded him that quickly, Jacquemart walked forward, looking to both sides as he searched the woods. He turned to the left and within mere feet of him was the woman, sitting on the ground with her back to him.

He acted precipitately, lunging forward onto the woman who sat unexpectedly.

He placed his large, rough hand around her mouth, preventing any chance of her screaming. The woman did not struggle until he jerked her body up to a standing position. His large, muscular frame offered no comparison to the woman's slender, petite body. With a show of his strength, he dragged her, like a dead boar, back through the woods.

Her eyes opened at the presence of a hand on her mouth. The hand was large, covering her nostrils, down to her chin. It pressed painfully, pushing her lips into her teeth, causing the taste of blood to spill onto her tongue. Piper was unaware of what exactly was going on as she kicked and gasped for breath through the tiny spaces between his fingers and her nose. She was not getting air. The moment was surreal, not because of shock but because she was lacking oxygen. Within minutes, the green leaves faded to a blur, until she saw nothing.

Jacquemart dragged Piper to the road. He looked to his right, then left, and spotted a car in the distance. He fell to the ground with Piper's limp body under his command. When the car passed, he stood up, picking up the limp body that, in his mind, was his mother.

Jacquemart dragged Piper over a mile until he was at his timber shed. He saw the wooden shelter and felt renewed strength. He kicked the door open and dragged piper inside. He pushed her body into the corner and pulled out the chair for him to sit on. Piper fell to the ground head first, face down.

"Why? Why did you do this to me?" he screamed at her. "Why would you give birth to me and put me into this world of torment?"

He did not receive an answer. He sat and waited for Piper to gain consciousness. After an hour, she began to moan softly. Jacquemart was watching as she slowly moved her arms, then her legs, and then rolled over onto her back.

"Get the fuck up," he yelled at her. "Get up you fucking cocotte and face me!" Jacquemart used the term he despised, cocotte, his stepmother's voice resonating in his head.

Piper did not hear what Jacquemart was saying. She only heard a man's voice, distant and discombobulated. She turned to her side and opened her eyes, thinking she was back at home in her bed, Nico lying beside her. She reached out to touch him, but she did not feel him. She was confused and realized that she was not in a bed. Her eyes focused on brown, worn work boots. She lay still trying to put the image into clearer focus. She followed the boots to the legs, then the waist, tee shirt, and Jacquemart's face.

"Lève-toi et répondez-moi, sale pute" (Get up and answer me, you filthy bitch"), he screamed to her in French.

She looked down at her hands that were bound with hemp rope around each wrist and tied together with four or so inches of rope. She looked at her ankles that were bound in the same manner. She looked at him and frantically tried to piece together the last several hours and make sense of everything. "I walked into the woods." She began to sift through the events, recalling the last action she remembered. "I must have passed out, but who's this? Where am I?" She looked around the timber walls of the shed. She looked down at the stone floor. "I must be in some sort of shed or cabin?" She looked at the man who was screaming to her in French.

"Je ne parles pas français." ("I do not speak French.") she screamed back at him. "What do you want from me?"

Jacquemart did not speak English. He stood up, grabbed her by the back of the head, and pulled her to her knees. He stood up and unzipped his pants. He realized that this was not his mother. Piper embodied all females and what he despised in them: their ability to have a man, any man, reduced to sex at their whim. The ability of a woman to have a child to a man she did not know reduced Jacquemart's entire existence to insignificance.

After unzipping the fly and unbuttoning the waist, he dropped his pants to his knees. Piper put her hands to the ground and tried to crawl away using her elbows. "No, no, no," she screamed.

Jacquemart grabbed her by the hair and pulled her back into position, on her knees, facing him. "Je bande pour toi (I have a boner for you). Suck my dick, you filthy whore." He pulled her head toward his stiff penis.

"No!" Piper screamed at him. She held her teeth together with her jaw clenched.

Jacquemart reached down into the pants that lay around ankles. He pulled out his wallet and opened it, pulling out a handful of Euros.

"Here, you filthy cunt. Does this change your mind?" He threw the money at her face.

She spit on him. "Fuck you," she screamed. "Putain de merde." Piper had learned French swear words from Nico.

Jacquemart looked at her and thought to himself, "Why is this whore not taking my money? Why isn't she sucking my dick?" He was confused.

Piper was still on her knees. She sat back on her side and rolled twice, taking her body to the wall. She sat with her knees under her body, wrists together on her lap. She was not crying. She was more consumed with anger than fear. "If he was going to rape me, he would have done it. If he was going to kill me, he would have done it." She looked at him without speaking, without moving her mouth or facial muscles.

A ray of sunlight found her face through the slates in the wood and angelically illuminated her cheeks and eyes. Her skin was clear and flawless. Her large brown eyes showed her emotion. Her large pupils screamed out to him with a look of sheer terror.

Jacquemart was not prepared for this response. He looked up at the large three-foot guillotine blade that he had rigged on the ceiling, suspended by ropes, and balanced by weights. He used the blade to split animals after the kill, when the meat was for the dogs. He looked back at Piper, bereft.

"I cannot kill her, not yet. She's a whore, a woman, she will eventually blow me. When she does, I will be prepared to punish her with death. Until then, she lives," he thought as he stood up and grabbed her by the twine in between her wrists. He picked her up and threw her over his shoulders, his right hand holding the rope in between her hands, his left hand holding the rope in between her ankles. The swift and unexpected move took Piper by surprise, forcing the air from her lungs and striking her in her solar plexus. She could not scream, only gasp for air, with each step he took.

Jacquemart was moving Piper out of the timber shed and into the château.

"I cannot think with this trash around me," he thought as he walked with her body to the dilapidated château. Piper lifted her head as her body lay draped around the stranger's shoulders. She was finally able to speak, "Where are you taking me?" she asked. Piper was unsure why the man was not responding to her. She knew he understood some of what she was saying. He was detached and unresponsive to her as if he was in a world of his own. She was merely a prop now, waiting, wondering, but all the while plotting to make her move and fighting to survive.

Jacquemart reached the château and walked around to the back of the house. Piper lifted her head to see a sideways view of a large, imposing limestone mansion. As they approached the château, she could see ornate stone arched dormers around the slate roofline. She wondered if anyone lived in the building; half of the long structure was missing a roof.

"I am being taken to an abandoned building to be killed," she screamed at him. "Stop! Where are you taking me?" She began to struggle with all of her survival instincts, posturing to fight for her life. As she screamed, she heard the sound of dogs barking. It sounded like hundreds of dogs, howling and barking. As she squirmed, Jacquemart tightened up the distance between her wrists and ankles. She continued to squirm, until he bent forward and threw her on the ground. Once again, all of the air was forced from her body. As she hit the ground, a piece of stone that was sticking up pushed into the back of her rib cage. She rolled onto her side in agonizing pain.

"Do you want to stay here on the ground? Should I let the animals eat at you?" he yelled at her in French. She did not respond. He reached down and picked her up, this time slinging her over his shoulder with her head falling down his back and her knees draped over the front of his chest. "Now, settle, you bitch," he said as he walked along the same route.

She lifted her head, but could only see the tree line from behind them and the small timber shed behind her. She tried to look around him, but was not able to see past his broad shoulders. In pain and exhausted, she collapsed forward. Each step was forcing air from her lungs and pressing down on her stomach and tender ribs.

"Oh God, what is happening? Why is this happening? What is he doing with me?" She tried to see how much room she had to move and possibly free her wrists. Every time she struggled, Jacquemart would throw her to the ground and repeat throwing her over his shoulder. To Jacquemart, she had no value. The only female that he valued was CeCeine, and now she was gone.

Piper lifted her head to view the woods as they grew more distant. "If I free my legs, I can run into the woods." She looked behind her again, trying to memorize the way back to the woods. She was not going to attempt fleeing now. She was tired, sore, and possibly bleeding. She made a survival decision to pick a better opportunity, when she had full strength.

She felt him stop and open a large wooden door with iron ornate hinges. He was carrying her into the château, across large black and cream marble tiles in a harlequin shape. It must have been a side entrance of some sort. Down the halls he walked, up a large, elaborate staircase with heavy ironwork displaying leaves and scrolls up the sides of the marble steps.

"Am I in an abandoned museum?" She thought as he took her to top of the stairs. She lifted her head wearily again. "Is this the part of the building that was falling down?" she asked as she turned her head to look up; it was not. She was trying to remember all the turns that he took as he meandered through the corridors and rooms.

He stopped again and opened another door. This one was painted white with small flowers framing the inside. He threw her body down; as she prepared for another hard surface, she realized that she had landed on a bed. It had linens. The room smelled musty, but was furnished and clean.

She sat up and asked Jacquemart once again, "What are you doing with me? What do you want?"

Jacquemart told her to shut up. He reached into his back pocket and grabbed a dog's pinch collar, prongs facing the inside, attached to a chain. "No, please do not put that on me," Piper begged him, but he did not understand or care. He placed the pinch collar on her neck, secured it with a small locking mechanism, and attached one end of a chain to the collar and the other to the bedpost. With every move, she made the prongs of the collar dig into her neck. She sat on the bed trying to plot a move, but was feeling faint. The man turned and walked out of the room. She could hear him locking the door from the outside. She did not have the strength to survey the room. She fell to her side and passed out, in part from sheer exhaustion and in part from the blows to her head. Before she could think another word, she was unconscious.

CHAPTER ELEVEN
CONFLICTED

Jacquemart walked down the hall, looking back at the locked door. He could hear his stepmother having sex, screaming wildly. He stopped to listen. Nothing. He did not hear a sound coming from the room. He continued to walk down the hall, past the seven bedrooms, down the stairs, and to the servant's room just off the kitchen. The fusty smell of grease and food hung in the air. He walked in and sat on the edge of the bed.

He strained his ears to detect whether he could hear his stepmother having sex in room above his. Jacquemart's lines of reality were blurring; he was living in a constant state of delusional mental torment. He saw Piper as his birth mother; at times, she took the form of his stepmother; and other times, as the whore in the park. He placed his head in his hands and grabbed his hair, pulling it, trying to get a grasp on his anger. He longed for the release he felt when he was plunging the knife into CeCeine; the blood that flowed onto the floor was a cathartic release of his emotions. Jacquemart lived a solitary life. His only communication with other people occurred when he conducted transactions with the hunters who commissioned his land. He would not deign to converse with individuals of lower intelligence or station. If there was one trait of the Dartmount name that Jacquemart carried on, it was the condescending air of aristocracy.

"I need a release." The voices in his head resonated and drowned out all other thoughts, causing him to act impetuously. He stood up and walked out of the room and the château, to his truck. He got inside and drove to the part of his land that bordered the whore park. He turned off his car and got out. He walked through the woods, scanning through the trees to see where they were standing.

Off in the distance, he could see the clearing where a group of women stood. He had never approached a woman before. Jacquemart was a virgin, insecure with every aspect of his being. He whistled as though he was whistling for one of his hounds. The group of prostitutes turned and looked into the woods. One of the girls in a mini skirt and tank top pointed into the trees and at Jacquemart, who was standing partially behind a tree. They talked for a moment and one of the women, a young black woman, started to walk into the woods toward him.

His heart pounded, palms gathered with sweat, and his chest tightened. He thought of running, but then felt a rush of blood to his penis. It was hard and erect. He was aroused at the thought of her mouth on it. He did not run; he stood against the tree, poised awkwardly as she drew near.

She called out to him, "Bonjour." He did not respond, but stepped out from behind the tree. He did not speak.

"What's your pleasure?" she asked him in French with an islander accent.

"Come with me," he replied. He walked back to his truck and the prostitute followed him.

He reached his truck and pointed. She continued to follow him. He got into the truck on the driver side and closed the door, not giving the prostitute instructions. She looked at him and assumed he was just shy. She got into the passenger side of the pickup truck. Jacquemart started the engine and put the truck into drive.

"Wait, I am not allowed to leave the park," she said urgently.

Jacquemart reached into his pocket and pulled out a wad of Euros. She saw the egregious amount of money and made the decision to go with him. Jacquemart drove to the timber shed. He pulled up and left the truck on for a moment as he thought of the possibility of this whore acting the same way as the last one had. He looked in his rear view mirror back to the bed of the truck. He had twine, pinch collars, and other items that could be used to gag, bind, and strangle if necessary.

Piper heard the vehicle. She opened her eyes, not sure whether she had dreamt the last several hours. She felt pain around her neck; she tried to feel her neck. Her hands were rubbed raw and bound. She tried to move her legs; her ankles were rubbed raw and bound. She lifted both hands and felt the metal collar that spiked into her neck. She had not dreamt the events that haunted her sleep, although she was at the point of exhaustion.

She sat up, and for the first time, cried. She cried tears of frustration, fear, and panic into her hands. She looked up and around the strange room. The bed had a huge ivory sheer canopy. The floor was made of large parquet wood squares. A large stone mantel with a mirror framed in ornate ivory painted wood. The mirror was as large as the mantle, reflecting all the grandeur of the room. She looked up and saw blue, gold, and red roses carved into the wood that framed the ceiling. The room had a large porcelain bowl and pitcher on one of the nightstands.

"Whose room is this? They must have been royalty." She looked around at the window where she had heard the car. She looked down at the chain attached to her collar. "There is enough room for me to make it to the window," she thought as she put her feet down onto the floor and shuffled to the window. She could stand inches away from it. The large damask blue and ivory drapes were ripped and stained. The window was thick glass that had bubbles in it. She tried to reach up to the iron scroll handle that kept the window closed shut. The window had a balcony outside of it.

"Maybe I can get outside the window and out onto the balcony." She felt hopeful for the first time. She reached out, but was too far to reach the handle. She stepped in closer and the prongs of the metal collar dug into her neck drawing blood.

She jerked back and grabbed her neck. She placed her finger to where the prong was lodged into her skin. She looked at her hand, red with her blood.

"If I do not remove this collar, I won't get out here." She felt the collar to see if she could remove it somehow. She could not feel how it was attached. She reached behind her neck and felt a small lock. She tried to open it without luck.

She heard a car door slam. Eyes wide, she looked back out the window, hoping to see if it was someone other than her abductor. She saw the tall stranger who had kidnapped her get out of the car and walk over to the passenger side door. He opened the door, turned, and walked away. A young black girl dressed in a short mini skirt and high-heeled shoes descended the truck and followed him. They both walked around to the front of the timber shed.

"He is not forcing her? Why is she following him in there?" Piper was confused. She watched, but could not see what he was doing inside the small building.

Jacquemart walked in and over to the small wood table at the far end. The young prostitute peered inside the dark shed. She looked down at the dirt floor covered with a woven hemp throw rug. The building was odd, and inside, even more so. The feeling in her gut was ominous. She was hesitant to follow him. Jacquemart sensed her reluctance and reached into his pocket to get his money. He pulled out the notes and grasped them tightly, rolling them into a wad that he then threw on the table. Seeing the money, the girl was inspired to walk in and count it. Jacquemart turned his back and unzipped his pants as she counted it. He turned to her with his pants down, penis limp.

"Get me hard and suck it—la flute." He grabbed his penis, "Biroute," he said as he offered his penis to her. He knew he would get hard; after all, this was a woman's role.

She was still counting the money, which was more than enough for oral sex. She folded the Euros up and placed them in a small nylon change purse that she wore around her neck. She zipped the purse shut and flung it to the back of her neck, allowing it to dangle down her back. She looked down at the dirty rug and placed her hands on the ground to brace herself as she bent to her knees. As she did, Jacquemart grabbed her by the back of her head and pulled her face toward him.

"Ouch," she said as she looked up at him. He was not smiling; his face was tense, eyes fixed on the floor underneath her. "Okay, calm down, big man," she said as she looked back down at his penis, which was now getting hard. She bent forward and placed her mouth on his penis.

"Right there, right there," Jacquemart said as he reached his left hand over to the wall. He did not move his eyes off the prostitute. He felt the air for the iron spike staked into the wall. The prostitute did not look up. As he moved, his penis fell out of her mouth. His free hand found the large spike; he unraveled the rope as he instructed, "Keep going." She placed her hands farther apart out on the floor and bent over to try to reach his dick. Jacquemart was beginning to orgasm prematurely from the anticipation and excitement.

"You filthy, dirty cunt," he said as he let the rope loose and stepped back from his spot on the carpet. A large metal blade fell from the ceiling. The prostitute did not have time to look up, move, or know what was happening. The blade slammed down onto her head as she bent over on all fours with her mouth open. Her head was severed from her neck and fell to the floor. Jacquemart sat down and continued to play with his penis. As he looked at her head, mouth and eyes open, he imagined her staring at his penis, and he came again. This time, he stroked harder, bringing him pleasure he had never experienced before.

He reached down, picked up her head, and wiped his cum off his penis with her open mouth. He kicked the rug back and exposed a small hole that had been dug underneath. He threw her head into the hole and covered it back up. He moved the table on top of it. He bent down and picked up the limp, headless body by the ankle and dragged it out of the timber shed.

Piper sat still looking out the window with countless thoughts flooding her mind as to the events ensuing in the timber shed. All of a sudden, she saw the man's back as he walked out of the timber shed. She looked with more intensity.

"He is dragging something behind him." She could not see what was on the ground by the way the truck was parked. She waited for the prostitute to exit. She did not. Piper watched.

Jacquemart bent over and picked up the body and threw it in the back of the pickup truck. Piper saw the mini skirt and tank top, now blood soaked.

"It looks like she does not have a head." Piper thought she was not seeing the body correctly. The body fell onto the bed of the truck, one arm tucked underneath and one out to the side. "Oh my God, she *doesn't* have a head," Piper gasped and ducked down, falling on the ground. "He can't see me. God, did he see me?" She answered confidently, "No, he did not look up; he did not see me." She crawled back to the center of the room where the bed was placed, and sat on the floor with her back poised against the side of the mattress. The decapitated body was not fully registering in her mind. She sat and stared into nothingness; her mind racing, she contemplated the possibilities.

"Oh my God, her head is missing. He cut off her head. He killed her." She placed her head onto her knees and shut her eyes tightly, hoping to erase the horrific sight from her mind. Every time she replayed the vision, she saw her own body. She had a pernicious premonition that this would be her.

She opened her eyes and thought, "I would not be here if it weren't for Nico, for his fucking indiscretions; God, why am I here?" She sat there directing her anger at Nico's actions. She sat in disbelief of the reality of her position.

"I will not die here. It is time for a game plan. Mis en place (put in place), Piper, prepare." She took a deep breath and found intrepidity victorious over the portentous possibilities that faced her.

CHAPTER TWELVE
LA BOUDOIRE DE MA MÈRE

Jacquemart severed the parts of the body as if it were any other carcass. The boars circled and called out for the meat as their snot noses lifted upward, catching whiffs of the blood that was spilling onto the ground.

The left leg was thrown into the pen of pandemonium, then the right. He continued until all the pieces were cut and fed to the passel of boars.

Jacquemart no longer felt the euphoric, intense dopamine rush. He was lethargic. He walked back to his truck and navigated through the woods back to the timber shed. He thought about his hounds; they did not feed upon the meat of his prey this time. He was saving the cocotte in his stepmother's bedroom for them. He opened the door, took a deep breath, stepped in, and sat down on the small wooden chair. He placed his head in his hands then laid his forehead on the table. Before he closed his eyes, he looked down as if looking through the rough-cut rudimentary table and onto the floor.

"Is she staring at me now?" he thought as he laughed sarcastically to himself.

He closed his eyes and allowed his body to rest for the time being.

Hearing the truck once again, Piper stood up. "Is he coming here?" she thought as she tried to determine the distance between her and the sound of the engine. She shuffled over to the window. The truck was back in front of the timber shed. She began to analyze the man's actions.

"He does not speak English; physically, he must perform manual labor; he is a large man and muscular. I will have to outwit him," she thought, trying to put together a profile for Jacquemart. "He is angry; has a fetish for prostitutes; lives in a run-down museum; has this one room immaculately kept. He is a fucking whacko." She could not profile him. "CSI, CSI... think, Piper. You have seen enough episodes. Okay, he is a loner, has some issue with whoever lived in this room, and, most important of all, did not kill me." She moved away from the window and sat on the floor by the bed. "Why didn't he kill me? I didn't have sex with him. That girl was obviously a prostitute. He wanted me to give him a blowjob. I didn't." She felt confident. "That's it."

She stood up and then lay on the bed, placing her head on the pillow. She slid the chain leash over so the prongs did not pierce her skin anymore than they already had.

"I'm starved." She was worried about her health, but was plotting and planning to save the fetus that was just developing in her stomach. "Do I tell him and try to prey upon sympathy?"

She did not have an answer yet. She was weak, hungry, and fatigued. Her eyes grew heavy, until she could no longer keep watch.

"He's coming," she said as she opened her eyes wide to the sound of keys jangling in the hall just outside of the bedroom. She looked out the window and noticed that the sun had disappeared. She looked at the frame and noticed the iron latch was not secured. She grabbed the chain, leapt out of bed, and shuffled as quickly as she could, falling onto her face. She could hear a key enter the lock of the door.

"I don't have time. I won't make it to the window in time. He will know I saw him." She rolled over to the window and stood up, locked it, fell to the ground, and rolled once before the door opened. She moaned to get his attention. "Ah, I am so hungry. Manger… hungry." She placed her hand on her stomach. The man walked over to her and lifted her body up off the ground and onto her feet. She felt a wave of panic and every nerve ending sparked.

Jacquemart reached out to touch her breast. Instinctually, she slapped his hand away. "No, don't touch me," she responded. He looked at her, confused. She reiterated, "Don't touch me," trying to think of the French words. "Touche pas," she yelled at him.

Piper wanted to survive, but the thought of this sick, demented stranger entering her and invading the sanctum of the womb that carried her child-to-be sickened her. She was not prepared to do this, not yet.

Surprisingly enough, he responded. He did not make another advance. She placed her hand on her stomach, "Please, I am hungry."

Jacquemart looked at her and did not understand. He noticed her hand on her stomach. She was not like the others. He was curious, yet skeptical of any possibility of virtuosity.

He turned and walked out without speaking. He was confused. For the first time, he did not see a whore, or his mother or stepmother; he saw a young, beautiful woman. He saw a woman who did not look like a whore—a woman that he did not recognize.

"What have I done?" he thought, not in a moment of regret but one of confusion. He walked out of the bedroom and locked the door from the outside. He walked down the hall, passing the oil portraits of his ancestors, judging his actions and failures. He stopped and looked at the portrait of his father; he gazed at it, turned, and kept walking.

"I am not a Dartmount," he said as he continued to walk. "I am the soul condemned to this hell."

He walked into the kitchen and opened the freezer chest. He pulled out a piece of meat. He looked at the frozen red disk and then threw it into the sink and walked out to feed the hounds. Jacquemart was aware that the meat was from CeCeine's loin.

"She wants food, let her eat another bitch."

CHAPTER THIRTEEN
JUST ANOTHER DAY

The heads of boars and red tailed deer looked on as Jacquemart sautéed the loin of CeCeine. Once it was cooked in a rudimentary style, he reached up and grabbed a plate from the cabinet, pulled it out, then set it back in place.

"Ma mère demands the Bawo & Dotter, Limoges porcelain." Jacquemart was once again hallucinating that Piper was his stepmother.

He walked over to the seventeenth century china cabinet and grabbed an emerald green and gold hand-painted porcelain plate. In the center of the plate was the Dartmount crest edged by gold and green grapes and vines.

He set it onto white linen with Laguiole silverware. He prepared a dinner plate as expected of him. Although several servants were hired to perform such menial tasks, Jacquemart was required to serve dinner to his stepmother in her bedroom, using only the finest Dartmount formal dinnerware.

He walked down into the cellar and selected a bottle of Mouton Rothschild. He looked briefly at the label to see that it stated 1945. He walked up the narrow stone steps back to the large kitchen. He slowly opened the bottle and set it aside to properly breathe. He looked down at the floor and wondered, "What will I have to tell her today? What will she have to scold me about? I did not talk to any girls. She asks me every day if I am still a virgin."

He looked at the tray and placed the meat on the plate, poured a glass of wine, and then a glass of water. He slowly walked the tray down the hall, up the winding staircase, and down the hall to her room. He set the tray on the floor and reached for the key.

Piper heard the keys striking together. She sat up, "Is he going to kill me this time?" She sat still, waiting for him to come in.

Jacquemart picked up the tray and walked into the room. He sat the tray down on the floor and picked up the linen napkin with the family crest embroidered on it. He placed it on Piper's lap. He picked up the tray and sat it down in front of her. She did not speak. She did not know what to say.

"Is he poisoning me?" She looked at the tray. A piece of seared meat sat in the middle of the most beautiful plate she had ever seen. A glass of red wine in a crystal wine glass and glass of water were placed adjacent to the plate.

"I am starving." She looked at the meat and could not help herself from picking it up with her hands and biting into it like an animal, ripping into the fibers with her bicuspids.

She wiped her mouth as juice from the meat ran down her chin. She picked up the water glass and drank its entire contents without so much as stopping for a breath.

Jacquemart did not make eye contact with her. He looked at the floor and turned his back to her while she ate. She looked at his back and wanted to speak, but was too thirsty and hungry.

"This is wild boar? Or deer?" she thought after she had eaten enough of the meat to calm her immediate ravenous state. "What kind of meat is this? It is brilliant, and prepared perfectly," she asked as she chewed, displaying manners not befitting her normal etiquette.

Jacquemart did not answer. He turned back around after ten minutes or so and picked up the tray. As he reached for the tray, Piper grabbed the glass of wine. She gulped the wine worth tens of thousands of dollars. She looked at him, feeling calmed that he was not judging her for eating in such a barbaric manner.

"Did you poison me?" She looked at him with an intense stare, realizing that he would not answer. To her surprise, he did.

"Non, Maman," he replied without looking up.

Piper, recognizing the word for "mother," did not know how to respond. She looked at him with perplexed eyes, mouth open, not speaking. "He thinks I'm his mum?" she thought to herself. "This guy is crazy." She did not say another word to him.

Jacquemart turned around, tray in hand, and walked out of the room, back the same route he had taken from the kitchen. He glanced down at his watch, realizing that he had a hunt in one hour.

The sun was setting early this time of year. This hunt was for a group of American hunters who had requested a stag hunt. He set the tray on the sink and left the house to gather his hounds, all the while thinking, "The maids will wash the dishes."

Jacquemart left the château with great haste. The kennels were around back, but the trailer was not hitched, and the dogs were not loaded onto the truck. He raced around back to the kennels. The dogs barked wildly at the sound of the truck. He backed up to the trailer, and with skill and efficiency, hitched it to the truck. He jumped back into the driver seat and backed the trailer up close to the kennel doors. He slid his legs out and stepped quickly around to the back. He opened the kennel and walked inside. The pack of dogs jumped up at him, yipping and licking their master. He selected the dogs that had the clean shaved "D" in their fur. This was the pack he was using for the month's hunts. He looked for the appropriate lead dog without stopping to contemplate the reason why CeCeine was not in the kennel.

He grabbed the dogs by their white tails and by the fur on the back of their reddish tanned necks; he lifted them as they stood rigid and threw them into the trailer. The dogs, 20 or so, landed one on top of the other without care. There were no windows in the small trailer. He slammed the doors shut and drove quickly through the meandering wooded road to the hunt site. It was a mere ten minutes away from the château.

He pulled the truck into the clearing by the stone wall to find the group of hunters in a circle, speaking to a police officer, un gendarme. He did not break a sweat. The sun had sunk low in the sky and the air was becoming chilled, combined with the day's moisture. He stepped out of the truck and pulled his collar up and around his neck and sunk his chin deep into his chest.

The lead huntsman called out when he saw Jacquemart, "Here he is." The pack walked away from the officer and toward Jacquemart, who did not ascertain the reason for the police being at the property.

The local police knew the Dartmount name and were familiar with the reputation of the recluse heir. There had not been a single disturbance in the last several decades.

"Jacquemart," the police officer called out, "Do you have a minute?" he asked of him.

"If you speak to me while I unload the hounds," he replied as he walked behind the trailer and unhitched it. Pushing out of the trailer was the pack of hounds, conditioned into routine that a hunt was imminent. The dogs circled around the hunters, noses to the ground, barking wildly, causing a vociferous auditory atmosphere.

"Jacquemart, one of the local prostitutes called in an abandoned car," he spoke while Jacquemart worked. "We searched the car and found that it belongs to an American on a vacation. It seems to be a sordid affair; her husband had a lover at the Hotel Courcelles and she left in some haste. We are investigating it. Have you seen a stranger or trespasser on your estate?" The policeman referred to the property as an estate in a fashion of great respect for the history and reputation of the Dartmount name.

Jacquemart did not look up. He walked to the small wooden crate placed outside the opening of the wall. Inside, a red tail male deer snorted and pawed at the floor.

"No, I have not seen anyone." He walked up the stairs to the rope that controlled the gate. "Non, Acel, I have not," he repeated, calling the officer by name. Acel was the name given to a male who was adherent of a nobleman. "Can you please pull up on the door to the crate?" he asked of him.

The police officer walked over to the crate and pulled the rope that lay behind the crate, and as he did, the door pulled up and the stag ran straight through the opening and into the walled parcel of land.

"I am sorry to interrupt you, Jacquemart. We have to check it out, as the car was at the cocottes' territory right outside of your land." After opening the crate, he stepped back and allowed Jacquemart to start the hunt.

Jacquemart opened the gate and allowed Cru, the dog he had selected to lead the pack in place of CeCeine, to lead the feverish hounds on the hunt.

"To the hunt," Jacquemart called out with a noticeable lack of zeal.

"To the hunt," the group of Americans called out as they all ran through the gate following the hounds.

Jacquemart walked back to his truck and opened the door. He sat down and turned his head back toward the policeman, "If I see her or anyone, I will let you know." He did not wait for a reply. He started his truck and slowly drove back to the château that appeared in front of him, suddenly, through the dark grey sky, as a dinosaur in ruins, standing tall.

It did not register to Jacquemart that the police were searching for the woman he had abducted from the park, for at that moment, she embodied his stepmother. He never gave the line of questioning a second thought. He answered with confidence, as he was confident, he had not met an American in the park.

CHAPTER FOURTEEN
THERE COMES A TIME

"Meet me in the morning; I will portion the stag then," Jacquemart said as he loaded the last hound into the trailer. The dogs were bloody and tired. It was acute to Jacquemart that he was running late, and he would have a penitence for that.

"Wait, what time?" one of the Americans called out as Jacquemart opened the door and got into his truck. Jacquemart rolled down the window and called back, "Eleven."

The American turned to one of his fellow hunters and said, "Hell, 11:00 is not morning in Texas. Shoot, we've fed, roped, and rounded by then." The two men laughed as they walked back to their pack.

Piper paced the room, studied her surroundings, took inventory of the surrounding grounds, and plotted her escape. She could not help but be curious of the behavior of her captor. She saw the level of his violence and rage. She could only assume that he was keeping her alive for some higher level of torture.

Her leash allowed her to reach as far as the window close to the bed and to the door that led to a large bathroom. A copper claw foot tub stood in the center of the room. A toilet and bidet stood off to side of the room. There were no sinks, just an ornate table with a large porcelain bowl in the center. The room had a screen that appeared to be hand painted flowers on silk fabric, and it was torn and faded.

Piper opened each of the drawers she could reach, to no avail. They were all empty. The baroque wallpaper that was peeling in every corner still held a vivid color of yellow and blue.

She stood in the bathroom, contemplating whether the room would offer aid in her escape. She did not hear the keys banging together—the standard alarm that the stranger was entering the room.

Jacquemart entered the room and took Piper off her guard. She jumped and let out a small scream as he walked into the bathroom holding a large pitcher. She turned and walked out of the room and sat back on the bed.

"I don't want him to think that I am plotting an escape," she thought as she quietly watched his actions.

He poured the contents of the pitcher into the copper tub and walked out. He repeated this act several times.

"He is filling the tub. He is going to drown me." She frantically looked around the room for an item to strike him with if he approached her.

Jacquemart walked over to the dresser that she could not reach by the length of her chain and pulled out a thin cotton dressing gown. He set the neatly folded gown on the end of the bed and walked into the bathroom and stood behind the silk screen.

Piper just sat on the bed looking at the dressing gown.

"What am I supposed to do? Put it on to be drowned?" She did not move.

Thirty minutes passed, and Jacquemart appeared from behind the screen, annoyed and seemingly agitated. He looked at Piper and then at the folded gown. He walked over to her and yanked her up off the bed. She screamed, "No," as she fought him. There was no match for the force of his weight against hers. He dragged her into the bathroom and threw her onto the stone floor. Her elbow spiked into the tile with all of her weight. She rolled to her side in pain.

Jacquemart grabbed the robe and threw it at her. He turned his back and folded his arms.

"He wants me to put this on. Do I do it, or get beaten around?" Piper had never experienced physical violence before, especially at the hand of a man. Nico was abusive verbally, but never physically.

She lay on the ground trying to plot the best strategic move. Jacquemart grew impatient with her. He walked over to her, grabbed the rope between her wrists, and pulled her up. He placed his hands on her shirt and ripped it off of her body, exposing her bra.

Piper folded her arms in front of her chest and screamed at him, "No, don't touch me." She started to cry as she squatted to the ground. "This is not happening," she repeated to herself.

Jacquemart picked up the cotton gown and held it up, unfolding it to full length. Piper made the decision that she would comply in order to avoid being hurt, disrobed, or even worse, raped.

She held her hands up and allowed him to put the robe over her head. "What the fuck is this psycho doing?" she mumbled as she sobbed. She did not take off her pants. She stepped into the tub and sat down in the warm water. She folded her knees and placed her forearms on them. As she cried, Jacquemart sponged her back with the warm water, then over her hair. When he was done, he stood up and picked up a towel. It smelled of damp must and was moldy. Piper cringed as he held it up in front of her.

When the strange bathing ceremony was complete, Jacquemart walked out of the room. Piper lay on the bed as if she had left her body and was watching a movie. She was numb to the reality of the events.

"Nico, where are you? Why is this happening?" she sobbed. She cried until she once again passed out.

It was at least a full day and night until she saw the stranger again. She was hungry and thirsty. The fillet was hardly enough for her and her child. It was going on five days without a meal or proper sleep, and unspeakable terror.

She walked over to the bathtub, stuck her head into it like a dog, and sucked the tepid, dirty water to quench her thirst. She was thankful she had, as she did not see a sink and couldn't bring herself to imagine drinking out of the toilet bowl that had likely not been cleaned in decades.

She woke to what she presumed was the next day, or even the day after that. Piper was losing track of the days. She was growing delirious.

"Mom, can I sleep with you and Dad tonight?" she asked into the quiet seclusion of her cell as she lay on her side, hugging the pillow. "There is someone in the attic; I am afraid," she said, as she could hear noises within the château walls. She was propelled to when she was a child, afraid of the attic door that opened up into her bedroom. She recalled lying in bed, imagining the handle turning slowly, as the door pushed slowly open into her room. She closed her eyes tightly. "Momma, hold me," she said, once again, in and out of consciousness.

The sun was bold and bright through the window, whispering to Piper to get up.

"Get up Piper; time for school," she heard her mother call to her.

Piper opened her eyes to the yellow and blue faded walls, ripped canopy bed, and locked door. She screamed for the first time, at top of her lungs, "Help me! Someone, help me! Please, someone, help me!" She fell out of bed, weak from lack of nutrition, and pulled herself over to the window. She stood and beat her fists on the glass.

"Help me!" She reached up and used both of her hands to turn the iron latch, pushing the window open and letting the cool air swirl into the room and across her face like a splash of water. She screamed out the window, "Help me! Someone, help me! P l e a s e, help me!" Nothing happened and nobody came to her aid. There was no white knight.

She turned and paced nervously. "Think, Piper. Pull it together." She hit the back of her hands onto her forehead. For the first time in days, it dawned on her, she was not trying to save herself; she was trying to save herself and her baby. She placed her hands on her stomach. "I promise, I will get us out of here."

She looked up and noticed, for some unprovoked reason, the corner of the wallpaper behind the bed. She looked closer and noticed a piece of something behind the small fold of the unglued wallpaper.

She shuffled over to the wall and fell forward to her knees. There was a small piece of paper behind the wallpaper.

"It's probably just the backing," she looked away and sat down with her back to the mattress, placing her head on her forearms that were placed on her bent knees. She looked up again at the piece of paper.

"Oh, what the fuck." She crawled over and started to peel away the old silk wallpaper. "This must have been gorgeous at one time. This bedroom is every woman's dream. I wonder what his mother was like." She thought about the possibilities as she peeled back the fabric from the plaster wall, disclosing an envelope.

She reached in, and with very little pressure, pulled at the envelope to dislodge it and release it from its seal.

"I wonder how long this has been here." She removed the envelope and turned it over. It was still sealed. She took her fingernail that was now broken but still sharp and loosened the back.

Slowly, she pulled it out. "It's a letter." The paper was thick and viscous. She opened the folds to disclose the letter, written using an ink well pen. "It's in French." She stopped and thought to herself, "Why would it be in any other language, Piper?"

The ornate penmanship was difficult to decipher. She tried to translate the words, her lips moving as she made an attempt to pronounce her way through the letters. "Je vis d'amour et d'eau douce," she mumbled. "I live on your love and water?" She looked up. "This is a love letter." For the moment, Piper was transported to a different place.

She turned the letter over and looked at the envelope. "When was this written?"

She deduced the age based on the ink pen and paper. She folded the envelope back up and placed it to her heart. "It is a letter of love, of hope."

She sat back and her eyes filled with tears. The reality of her situation and of her marriage, and the fate of her unborn child all collided within her mind.

"Nico, I love you. I love you more than I have ever expressed to you. I am sorry for that. I wish I would have told you more." She held the letter to her heart as she lay on her side, on the hard floor, staring out into the quiet, unfamiliar room.

Once again, sadness overwhelmed her as she thought, "The person for whom this letter was meant never got it. Why do we go through life and relationships holding back?" She cried openly, "Would this letter have made a difference in her life?"

CHAPTER FIFTEEN
UNRAVELING

"Nico Blanche," said Nico with eyes down as he placed his black Hermes attaché on the marble counter at Hotel Courcelles.

With a startled look on his face, the young woman behind the desk looked up at Nico.

"Une minute, Sir," she said in her English dialect. Her short response was noticeable and aberrant from the usual level of professionalism at this particular hotel. She quickly walked away and through the glass doors that led to the manager's office. Nico had not spoken to Piper or Nicole. Nicole had not spoken to anyone back at the Petite Piper about the incident with Piper. She was intentional in her actions to not have Nico hear of the incident, as she did not want to return to the States or derail her holiday with Nico.

Nico looked up then into the office where the young woman was placing a phone call. He continued to watch her movements. She did not speak to anyone, and then, she hung up the telephone.

"Excusez-moi?" Nico yelled out. "I have just arrived from a very long flight from the States, and I would appreciate you waiting on me now," he demanded.

The young woman looked at Nico and walked out of the office, smoothing down her black skirt as she walked.

"I am sorry for the delay, Monsieur Blanche. There was a slight episode here yesterday."

"Episode? What kind of episode?" Nico grew incensed with every minute.

"It seems your wife checked in, before your female companion." The desk clerk attempted to be discrete, yet to the point.

"What are you talking about? Piper? Piper was here?" A wave of shock flowed over Nico. He never expected to hear this news.

"Yes, Mrs. Blanche checked in. We escorted her to her room, and then, a Miss Nicole Blanche checked in after her."

"Did the two speak?" Nico asked.

"Yes, monsieur," replied the young woman.

"Where did Piper go? Where did Nicole go?" Nico was now yelling as he raked his hands through his tussled hair.

"Ms. Nicole is in the room. Mrs. Blanche checked out, in quite an enraged state." She downplayed the incident to Nico.

"Take me to my room," Nico said as he collected his personal items.

"May I please have your American Express card that you used when placing the reservation? I will swipe the card."

Nico interrupted her as he reached back into his back pocket and pulled out his wallet, "I know the procedure, and I did not make the reservation; my personal assistant did." He did not look up as he shuffled through several credit cards before selecting the black American Express card. He threw it on the desk, "Swipe it and send it to my room with a bottle of Bordeaux, preferably Château Mouton Rothschild."

He turned and walked away without waiting for the young woman to respond. He pushed the door open and slammed it shut as he mumbled his final words, "Go on, swipe the card and have it sent to my room. If there is anymore conflict let me know immediately."

The employee called out, "Certainly, Monsieur Blanche," as Nico walked out of the room. She quickly raised her hand and motioned for the bellman waiting outside to enter the lobby.

"Take Monsieur Blanche's credit card to him, and take a bottle of Bordeaux, on the house." She swiped the card and handed it to the young employee, who was inexperienced in dealing with such a situation.

Nico knocked on the door, not waiting for the bellman to accompany him to his room. "Nicole?" He knocked again.

The door opened to a teary-eyed woman, blonde hair pulled back, white silk robe covering a white silk halter negligee.

"Oh, Nico, I am so glad you are here. It was horrible." Nicole threw her arms around Nico's neck. He hugged her back as he stepped her backwards into the room. She walked backwards on tip toes without loosening her grasp of his neck.

"What happened, Nicole? Why didn't you call me?" he asked sternly as he removed her arms from around his neck.

"I arrived as planned and checked in. That's it. Piper, for some reason, was already here. They thought I was some drifter trying to scam a room. It was so humiliating. I had to actually confront her, well, sort of. She was so abusive; it was horrible," she explained her version of the story with great emotion.

"What did she say to you? Did she say why she came?" Nico was trying to ascertain more about Piper than Nicole was professing.

Nicole changed her demeanor. "Nico, the bitch showed up, called me a whore, and said she wasn't staying. She left. That's it." She turned and sat on the bed and crossed her legs. Just as

Nico began to speak, the front desk employee showed up with a tray, two glasses and a bottle of wine, and the bellman.

"Excusez-moi, Monsieur Blanche, your wine and credit card." He walked into the room. "May I open it for you?"

Nico nodded in affirmation and the young man uncorked the wine. He picked up the bottle and read the label aloud, "Château Monbousquet, 2005. Just one bottle?"

The room fell awkwardly quiet as the bellman placed Jacquemart's suitcase on the wooden rack.

"Shall I uncork it for you, Monsieur?" the bellman asked again as he pulled out a bottle opener from his back pocket.

"Of course," Nico replied arrogantly.

The bellman lifted the knife from the cork screw and removed the foil from the bottle. He nervously uncorked the bottle as the cork squeaked out of the bottle. He turned and handed the cork to Nico for inspection. Nico held it to his nose and smelled the cork. He placed the cork to his lips and felt it to ascertain its condition of saturation. After he performed a thorough inspection and was satisfied, he handed the cork back to the manager. The elderly man poured the wine into the large balloon shaped glass and handed it to Nico. He swirled the wine around and placed his nose into the rim as Nicole, the bellman, and the young front desk employee looked on.

"It's fine," he said as he wiped his mouth after swirling it around his tongue.

"The Bordeaux is on the house, Monsieur Blanche," the front desk man replied, "with our apologies." He insecurely looked away as he spoke to Nico.

Nico looked him squarely in the eye. "Merci. Now, please, leave me, all of you."

The two left and the door closed shut. Nico walked over to the wine and poured a full glass. He drank it down without stopping for a breath of air. He set the glass down and then he sat on the chair.

"Nicole, what did Piper say when she left?"

"She said I was a whore, Nico. Does that bother you at all? Oh, and she said, 'I hope you two are happy.' Now can we focus me and not her?" Nicole stood up and took off her robe.

Nico looked at Nicole in all her young, soft firmness and thought of his ego.

"Ma petite chérie, I just want to know what happened. I am sorry that happened to you. Here, have a glass of wine." He poured her a glass of wine, all the while plotting his best plan.

Nico thought, "Piper is my wife. She gets mad, blows off steam, but is always there for me. Nicole, she is not so addicted to me. I need to cultivate this one longer. Piper will go home, be mad, get on with it, and I will see her when I return. I will send her a dozen lilies, bon."

He turned to Nicole. "My little one, I am sorry for this." He picked her up off the bed and hugged her. "Shhh, it will be alright. We will have a wonderful time here in Reims."

Nicole smiled and hugged him back. She was satisfied, as she had heard the answer she wanted. The room had a strange aura about it, if one was open to sixth senses, of Piper's pain, the love she felt for Nico, and the hurdle she had scaled when she decided to write the letter from the desk in the corner—the letter that was lost in transit.

Nico placed his hands on Nicole's tight, tanned thighs and slid his hands up until he reached her young, firm ass. She lifted her legs and wrapped them around his waist as he fell backward onto the bed.

"Monsieur Blanche," said a voice, followed by a knock at the door, interrupting Nico briefly. The knock continued and was again followed by the calling out of his name.

"Fuck!" Nico screamed out. "What now?" He got up off of the bed and walked over to the door. "What?" He shouted.

"It is the police. Please open the door."

Nico looked shocked. He obeyed and opened the door and looked out at two French policemen. "What is going on?" he asked.

"We need to ask you some questions about your wife." The second of the two glanced through the door and into the room at Nicole. "Is this Mrs. Blanche?" he asked in a sarcastic tone.

"Nicole, please go and turn off the shower," Nico called out to her, hoping she would pick up on his ruse. "No, it is not. This is one of my chefs."

"Well, your wife's rental car was found abandon a few miles from the hotel. Her luggage, purse, and passport were inside. Can you tell me why she left?" the first police man asked sternly.

"Piper was not scheduled to be in France with me. She arrived and went home to attend to our restaurant business after realizing she was not needed here." Nico was firm and confident with his answer.

"That's quite contrary, Monsieur Blanche, to the story we were told by the hotel staff. I understand that she left after finding out your lover had attempted to check into this room. Is that her, the lover?" The police officer cocked his head and his eyes, looking at the bathroom as if he were judgmentally glaring through the walls at Nicole.

"Please, come with me," the head officer asked Nico.

Alarmed and paranoid, Nico responded perfunctorily, "Where and why? What the fuck is going on?"

"Just come with me, Monsieur Blanche." The officer opened the door to the suite and walked out and down the pea gravel path, past the century old statutes that seemingly cast their glare upon Nico as he walked in the shadow of the officer to his patrol car.

The officer reached his car and opened the door. He pulled out Piper's Hermes purse. "Is this your wife's?" he asked Nico.

"I don't know. She has so many bags." In all honesty, Nico did not know what bag Piper was carrying these days.

The officer pulled out her passport and showed it to Nico.

"Is this your wife's passport?" He looked at Nico in a very discerning manner. He thought to himself, "It is sad that this man's wife is missing and he can't identify her belongings. His lover's purse, I am sure, was bought by him." He could not hide his dislike of Nico. "Monsieur Blanche, is this your wife's passport?" He raised his voice and opened the booklet to display her photograph.

Nico looked at the picture and replied, "Yes. Why?"

The officer became annoyed. "Monsieur Blanche, as I stated already, we found her rental car, abandoned. Her belongings, as you see, are intact. We suspect foul play. Do you have any idea what happened?"

"No, I just arrived. I am tired. I am a celebrated chef, or don't you know me? I am Nico Blanche. I am here to participate in the opening of France's highest Michelin rated chef, Monsieur Boucharnte. I was told my wife left to go back home to the States. I have not spoken to her."

"Look, Blanche, your wife, at this time, is considered at risk of foul play. I suggest you go back to your mistress and stay put. Do not leave the country until otherwise advised." He stared at Nico.

Nico stared back and then replied, "I may have given you the wrong impression. I love my wife. I am tired. All this news was just placed on my lap within an hour of my arrival in France. I have not slept. I will fully co-operate with whatever it is you ask of me. I am sure Piper went home and is fine. Here are the phone numbers of the restaurant and our home." Nico motioned for his pen and pad. He wrote down the telephone numbers. "I have no intention of going anywhere." He closed the leather bound note pad and handed it back to the officer. "Now, may I return to my suite for some rest?" He looked at the officer with a simulated concerned look.

"I know where you will be, Monsieur Blanche." The officer escorted Nico from the patrol car and watched him walk back to the room.

Nico passed the second officer on the way, "Bonne nuit," he said as he passed him on the narrow path. The second officer did not reply.

Once both officers were in the car, they looked at each other. The senior officer spoke, "He is our main suspect. The pompous bastard, I will admit though, makes a decent pate." The two officers laughed as they fastened their seat belts and drove away from the hotel.

Nico knocked on the door, "Nicole, it's me, Nico. Open up."

Nicole opened the door. "Oh my god, Nico, what is going on? Do you think something happened to Piper? Maybe she killed herself over me and you?" She spoke with sincerity and over-inflamed naïve confidence.

"Don't be silly, Nicole. She is fucking with me. She went home. This is her form of punishment toward me." He sat on the bed and unbuttoned his shirt. "Pour me another glass of wine," he demanded.

Nicole credulously obeyed. She handed the glass to Nico and the door once again sounded with a knock.

"Oh, what the fuck now? Nicole, get the fuckin' door," he screamed at her.

Nicole opened the door to find two hotel employees—the young woman from the front desk and a man.

"Yes?" Nicole asked.

"May we speak to Monsieur Blanche, s'il vous plait?" she asked, clearing her throat.

"Nico, they want you," Nicole yelled out in annoyance as she walked away.

Nico did not get up off the bed. He drank the wine that Nicole had poured for him. "What now?" he asked, looking up briefly to acknowledge their presence.

"May we speak to you in private?" the female employee asked Nico.

"No, ask me what you need to so I can go to bed," he replied.

"I understand that the police were here tonight. I must notify management, Monsieur Blanche." She looked at Nico trying to exert the authority that she held in the absence of the manager and assistant manager. The employee accompanying her did not speak; he merely looked on as if he was there purely for moral support.

"I am tired, I have done nothing wrong, and I am asking you once to leave us alone." Nico stood up and unbuttoned his shirt.

"I am sorry to inconvenience you, Monsieur Blanche, but we have corporate directives that must be followed," said the young woman as though she was reading from cue cards.

"'We?' Who the fuck are 'we'?" Nico stood up and took off his shirt. He walked closer to the employees and stood within inches of their faces, as if he was one of his insubordinate chefs.

"Monsieur Blanche, please step back, dress, and meet me outside the room," she said firmly as she stepped back and turned her back to the open door.

Nico stepped back and said, "I will see you in the morning. For the rest of the day, I am going to relax and sleep." He slammed the door shut and moved the lock bar across the frame, locking the door.

The young employee looked at her co-worker. "I have to call Monsieur Jardine. I won't pay hell for this pompous prick." She walked away from the room as her co-worker replied, "This guy is a fuck head." They both laughed and walked down the path back to the lobby.

Nico was filled with the contentment of victory, as usual. He started to walk back to the bed, but stopped and smelled the air. As a chef, he had an acute sense of smell. He looked around the room and felt a strange, overwhelming sense of familiarity.

"I smell Piper," he thought. "This is the sweet aroma of Piper's scent."

He sat down on the bed, and it struck him, something had gone wrong with his selfish, shallow plan. He looked over at the desk and noticed it was open. A pen was out and a piece of stationery was left on the table. He glanced and looked away as Nicole spoke to him.

"Nico, let's get out of this shithole. We don't need to stay here. There are other hotels in France, right?" She spoke with the innocence and ignorance of an American on her first trip to Europe.

"Nicole, not now." Nico was drained. "We will stay here. I am Nico Blanche. I do not get thrown out of hotels." He walked over to the bottle of red wine and poured himself another glass. He reached into his wallet and pulled out a wrapper of white powder.

He sat at the desk and poured the cocaine onto the wood surface. He pulled a random credit card out of his wallet and cut himself a large line of the drug. He picked up the pen— the same pen that Piper had used—and unscrewed the cap. He removed the ink capsule and spring. He bent down and snorted the line through the pen, sat back in the chair, and took a drink of the Bordeaux sent by the manager. "Let them all fuck themselves. I came here to cook. Piper is Piper; I will not tarnish my reputation in my home country. Now, come, Nicole, sit on my lap."

Nicole giggled and pranced across the room to plop her firm buttocks down on his lap and place her tongue in his mouth.

CHAPTER SIXTEEN
SUN IN VERSAILLES

She swallowed slowly, sucking the saliva from under her tongue. She did not lift her head off the pillow. Her eyes were fixed on the large ornate mirror ahead, reflecting the silk canopy and hand-carved bedposts. The oil canvas portrait behind the bed reflected in the mirror, looking almost as if it was her reflection staring straight ahead into the gilded mirror. Long grey hair was placed meticulously upward, long slender neck flowed down into a crimson red silk ball gown that wrapped around her slender shoulders. A large diamond and ruby necklace dangled from her neck into a deep V with teardrop diamonds surrounding the tip.

The woman's lips were well formed, yet the soft brush strokes softened them into a slight smile. The bridge of her nose was perfectly straight and thin, and her almond eyes were amber brown.

The woman gazed out at Piper as if she wanted to tell the secrets of the grand bedroom. Piper just stared, thirsty, starving, and growing weaker and more delusional with every passing hour. Off in the distance, she could hear a piano.

It was her father. She sat up and walked over to the door. She peered around the corner and saw his back at the black shiny grand piano, moving to the left and right, enveloped in the music. He was playing Bach's Goldberg Variations. She tiptoed into the room and lay behind the bench on her back, arms folded under her head, listening.

"Piper Florence, are you spying on me?" The music stopped, although he did not turn his back.

Piper giggled and leapt to her feet to hug his back, although her arms did not reach fully around the tall, handsome man.

"Come, play with me. You know this song." He perched her up on the stool and continued to play as her right hand joined in.

Piper smiled and looked over at her dad, "Tell me again why my middle name is Florence." Her Dad did not answer. "Dad," she called out.

She looked to her left, but only saw the vanity table at the far end of the room with the ornate tapestry seat.

"Florence is for the town in Italy, where your mother and I conceived you, under the warm summer sun. It is beautiful, Piper, just like you," she whispered out into the stillness of the quiet bedroom.

"Papa, you'd love this bedroom. It's classic and proper and beautiful." Tears filled her eyes and flowed onto the linen pillow. The music started again; the piano flowed through the notes of the introspective melody, slow and soft, then lively and loud.

Piper was a lover of all that was classical, historical, and architectural. This, she learned from her father, the man she grew up adoring. Her lively spirit was a gift from her mother, but her courage, compassion, and spirit were all gifts from her father.

Piper loved period films, imagining herself as the heroine in all of them. She traveled throughout Europe visiting historical homes and castles, as her father wanted her to do.

Strangely enough, she now lay in awe of her surroundings, although she was a prisoner. Each day that she survived, she felt the chances of getting out of the beautiful cell were greater.

She placed her hands on her stomach, and said, "Please hold on with me. I will get us out of here." She conserved her energy and did not lift her head or get up. She lay waiting to hear the sound that she both loathed and, ironically, longed to hear: the keys striking together in the hall.

"Knight, I will name you Knight. One day, we will listen to Papa's favorite, Goldberg Variations, together." She closed her eyes and heard the music again.

She opened her eyes and saw Nico lying beside her, stroking her hair. She smiled. "Nico, I had the worst nightmare." She began to tell him, "Nicole, that ditzy server, was in France. We fought. I was driving to another hotel to get away from her and went to the woods to pee—I know, classless—I could not help it. I had to go really badly. Anyhow, this guy abducted me and took me to this strange derelict château, and…"

"Shh, ma chérie," he said as he stroked her hair. "Open your mouth." He kissed her lips softly and then placed a piece of Maison du Chocolate onto her tongue. The soft, bittersweet hazelnut flavored ganache slowly melted, filling her mouth with a sweet, lasting taste.

Piper was transported back to her first official date with Nico. She was working in the pastry kitchen at the restaurant Nico owned, performing a stage set up by the pastry school she was attending in Philadelphia. Piper was immediately attracted to Nico and him to her. The clamorous kitchen was an exciting and passionate setting for their chemistry. They exchanged personal stories while on breaks, sitting at the small table outside the kitchen, drinking lemon verbena tea.

"I have arranged for you to have tomorrow off," Nico said to her. "Meet me here at 9:00 A.M."

Piper met him as agreed. He drove her to a small stable in the neighboring village to the restaurant. Out in front of a field and stone stable were two large, saddled horses.

"Oh my God, Nico, they are beautiful. Are we going riding?" She laughed with delight as she turned to him, leaned over, and kissed his cheek. "I do not have riding clothes."

Nico reached around and grabbed a large white box with a green satin ribbon tied around it. "This is for you," he replied as he handed her the box.

Piper untied the bow and lifted off the top of the box to reveal a pair of black tweed riding britches, socks, and a white blouse with a green ascot.

"And you know my size, Mr. Blanche?" She looked at him with slight hesitation. "I hope they are not too small." *He will think I am a large ass*, she thought to herself as she cringed, looking at the size of the pants. "They are the right size," she said, surprised and impressed. "How did you possibly figure out my size, Nico?"

"You underestimate my personal assistant, Claire." They both laughed.

"There is one more problem," she said as she looked at him, her face beaming. She pointed to her high-heeled mules.

"Ahh," he uttered and pointed to the back seat, "But again, Claire it is bonne (good)."

She reached around and pulled forward a pair of black and brown perfectly stitched riding boots.

"Now, I will die if you have this one right," she said to him with a large smile.

"Seven. You forget, she ordered your kitchen clogs," he said as they both laughed. "Now, ma chérie, les cheveaux await. Tout de suite."

The pace was quick as the two galloped through the French countryside. The horses' long black manes lifted into the air and flowed in the wind as they ran through the minutes of the day. The ground was firm and the hooves of the horses kept rhythm with Piper's heartbeat. She used her skill and athleticism to keep stride with Nico. She breathed in and smelled the cool air. Ahead of them, the sun was high and bright in the summer sky, displaying the neighboring vineyard that was gloriously lush and green with light green grapes dangling from every branch.

Nico stopped pace and Piper followed suit. He dismounted the horse and stepped forward to grab hold of the reins of her horse.

"Why are we stopping, Nico?" she asked.

Not answering, he walked the horses toward the rows of grape vines. Off in the short distance, she could see a group of three men. They were dressed in black pants and crisp white shirts, with towels draped over their arms.

A large, thick, ivory and blue blanket covered the ground. Three large wooden picnic baskets sat at the end.

"Are we having a picnic?" she asked. She thought to herself, "I could never have imagined this perfect day, with this perfect man; this is a dream."

She could still see the card that one of the waiters handed her,

Ma Marie Antoinette
Cocktail Dubarry
Aloyau à la Dauphine

Canard avec prune
Fraise au lait
Chocolate
Ville d'avray
Chateau de Reignac Blanc
Chateau Monbousguet

Piper recognized the menu as some of Marie Antoinette's favorite foods. During some of their many talks, she had spoken of her love for the "misquoted and misunderstood queen."

The two dined, laughed, fed one another, and lay in the sun until it traveled through the sky to end their single perfect day.

"Nico, tell me again of the moon shape of the croissant," she asked.

There was silence.

"Nico, don't deny me the story. Just one more time. P l e a s e?" she sounded like she did when she would ask her father to play and replay Bach on his piano.

Nico did not answer.

She opened her eyes to the faded wallpaper. She sat up for the first time. "Nico?" she called out.

Suddenly, it dawned on Piper, she had dreamt the entire replay of the day. She looked out the window into the darkness. She closed her eyes, tears no longer capable of being shed, as she was dehydrated and weak.

Suddenly, she heard the dangling of the keys. "Am I imagining this also?" she thought, afraid to trust her mind.

She heard the sound again and the door creaked open. She sat up and saw the figure of her abductor. She was not imagining it.

In walked Jacquemart carrying a bottle with a porcelain-hinged top, filled with water. He walked over to her and sat her up. He poured the water into her mouth.

She choked and gasped as she gulped the water. He stopped when the bottle was half empty. He hinged it shut and set it on the floor by the bed. As he set it down, he noticed a faded envelope in Piper's left hand. He looked at her; she did not move. She was still coughing and gasping for air. He removed the letter from her hand.

"My family crest, in wax? Qu'est-ce que c'est? (What is this?)" He looked at the envelope and back at Piper, then back at the envelope. He did not open it. He picked up the lantern housing a candle and walked over to the window to examine the seal. He held it up to the flame. The hardened red seal clearly displayed a D that circled around the top and squared around the arches.

Jacquemart looked down at the ring on his middle finger of his right hand, where he wore the gold ring bearing his family crest. This ring was also used to make the imprint of the family crest that he was holding in his hand on a letter that he had never seen before this moment. He twirled the ring as his mind pondered the possibilities.

"This is my family's seal," he said as he turned and looked at Piper, who had stopped coughing and was back on her side, holding her stomach. For the first time, he looked at her and actually saw her movements. They were the movements of an American stranger, not his stepmother, not a prostitute, but an unknown person. He watched her as she rubbed her stomach and cradled it with her hands.

"She holds her stomach like she is protecting it," he thought. "This woman is with child."

Jacquemart began to feel warm; his forehead collected with several small beads of perspiration. He carelessly wiped his brow with the back of his hand as the room began to spin. He looked around the room as he reeled back. "Where did she find this?" He looked at the furniture. "I have been through each piece of furniture in this room. He looked at the floor to see that none of the carpets were turned back. His eyes searched the pictures and any other piece of furniture that her leash would allow her to reach.

He did not see anything out of order. He looked back down at Piper and stared at her face. She was growing very pale.

"This strange American may have been sent to release me—release me from this miserable perpetual prison of torment." He turned and walked toward Piper, carrying the lantern. He set it down onto the nightstand and leaned in toward her.

"Is she an angel?" He leaned in closer to see her soft eyes, pale white skin, and soft curly hair.

He reached into his pocket and removed his keys, searching for the small key that fit the lock on her collar. He placed the key into the lock and released the tortuous shackle from her neck. Piper stirred, but did not wake.

Jacquemart dismissingly looked at the dried blood that had crusted around the puncture holes encircling her neck. He dropped the collar to the ground. The chains rattled as it struck the limestone floor. Piper shifted to her back, her right hand still cradling her abdomen. She did not open her eyes.

Jacquemart lifted the lantern and walked out of the room without looking back. His mind was on the obscure letter, the angelic American, and her fetus. His rush of realization evoked in him a lack of rational thought or compunction for Piper, who, in reality, was falling deeper into a dangerous state of shock.

CHAPTER SEVENTEEN
INHERITING TORMENT

Jacquemart walked out of the château and down the path to his timber shed—the only place he could bring himself to feel the safety and comfort he would need to bring himself to read the contents of the strange, antique letter.

His entire childhood to his adult years were molded by the lies and propaganda fed to him by others for self-serving motives. His father denied the truth that he was stuck with a title that solidified his fate and denied him his one true love. His stepmother despised the fact that her husband slept with a prostitute who gave birth to a bastard son who she was forced to raise.

After several reflective moments, and reticence, he unfolded the aged linen paper to read the letter that would reveal the truth about his life.

The letter read,

Odette,

I look into thy immortal grey eyes and see the great pain that is forthcoming. Do not let me lure you—Freedom, do not taunt me. I know well the terms of loss, piling up and overwhelming my weary mind, for my enemy knows my every move. I see the events unfolding upon me. Control this life, I cannot, though my weak fists grab at every minute I have with you, my love. This elusive moment suffocates me, compressing my chest, forcing the breath from my being.

Can I catalogue your smile, your graceful movements? Can my cluttered mind hold all of the visions that I cling to?

My words are the interwoven stitches of this tapestry. As I place pen to paper, they are fading and tottering. I have fruitlessly tried to shelter thee from standing at this gate.

In this short time, you have gifted me. Your being creates every moment of this elusive, fleeting euphoric state. Remember this warmth when the cold, bitter reality stings your heart and pains your sweet soul. Remember me, as I whisper further, until I am at a far.

My angelic Odette, you were sent to release me, though fleeting. My heart flew free and soared above, looking down on a pathetic existence. But rejoice, for I am finally free.

In Perpetum,

Adrian

Instead of having a change of heart toward his mother, he became enraged. "My father did not love my mother?" Although the words were filled with love, regret, and heartache, Jacquemart remained in a state of denial.

"My mother was nothing more than a street whore. My father was the blood of aristocracy." His rage augmented with his incongruent thoughts. "She tricked me. The American wrote this."

He folded the letter back up, placed it back in the envelope, and set it on the table. He looked around at the timber walls shedding the new light of day. He had not slept. He felt uncontrollable and insatiable aggression.

He looked down at the newly arranged dirt that covered the resting place of the young prostitute's head. He drew the mucus from his lungs and spit it on the makeshift gravesite.

His eyes scanned the room as he searched for the small cattle prod he used to control the boars. He spotted it and walked over to pick it up. He placed the tool in his back pocket and then kicked the door open with his boot.

"It's time to perform my duty," he thought as his feet pounded the ground, keeping pace with his heart rate.

"Fucking whores, fucking whores, fucking whores," he repeated incessantly with every step.

He finally stopped and squatted down, placing his head in his hands, applying pressure to his forehead with his fingers, trying to control his thoughts and the conflicting voices in his head. He heard what his father said, what his stepmother said, and now, the words on paper from his own father's hand.

"Father did not love that woman." He tried to push the thought of love from his mind with his hands pressing on his skin. "He did not love that woman," he repeated.

He stood and continued walking down the path until he reached the spot where he had found the last prostitute.

The park was now his hunting ground.

"Where are they?" he asked as he crouched in the brush, looking and waiting for his prey.

He saw a black Ford arrive. The door swung open, and three young women jumped out, laughing and talking with one another as they slung small purses around their shoulders. He watched and waited until the car drove off.

The group of girls walked from the pull-off area and over to the trees. One of the girls pulled a plastic bag out of her purse and looped it over one of the trees. Jacquemart watched and mumbled to himself, "Fucking cum catchers."

He was aware that the local police allowed the whore to assemble on this plot of wooded land. The girls stood off into the trees in an attempt to be discrete. The plastic bags were for trash, mainly used condoms. If the prostitutes followed the rules set by the locals, they were left to solicit.

Jacquemart was calculated and patient as he looked around to pick out the right one. He wanted one who was light skinned; he wanted a French woman who resembled his mother.

"Come on, little whore," he said as he watched, "Come to me."

He imagined his mother seducing his father. "He was weak and pathetic," he thought.

Minutes grouped into hours and elapsed as he waited, until finally, the one prostitute he hunted walked away from the group. He popped up and stepped out and away from the brush. He whistled loudly at her and she looked over at him.

She walked toward him. Jacquemart did not speak. He cupped his hand to this groin with his legs wide. He smiled at her as he stood his ground.

"Come to me, little whore," he thought with a plastic grin on his lips.

The prostitute walked over to him, noticing his stature.

"He is very handsome, and big," she said to herself as she approached him. The prostitutes were accustomed to truckers pulling off the road, tired, dirty, usually overweight and unkempt.

"What's your pleasure, darling?" she yelled out.

Jacquemart did not speak to her; he merely gestured with his head in affirmation that he wanted her services. He wanted her.

The young French woman walked over to him with unusual anticipation that this one would not be so perfunctory.

Her name was Onnette and she was a sex addict. She felt a sense of drug-like euphoria when having sex. Emotionally, when she was having sex, she felt needed and had a sense of belonging that was lacking in her life.

Onnette was unlike the other prostitutes; she enjoyed the intercourse that was part of her job. As she walked to Jacquemart, her groin ached with anticipation of the imminent sexual act.

Once she was within inches of Jacquemart, the first thing she noticed about him were his dark, intense eyes.

"Hello," she said.

Jacquemart reached into his back pocket and removed the cattle prod. He remained calm, held his ground, waited, smiled, and then quickly and firmly, he pressed the cattle prod into her neck.

Onnette's body reverberated from the jolt and then slumped to the ground. Jacquemart reached down and picked her limp body up off the ground and threw her over his shoulders.

He started his trek through the woods, carrying her along the same path as he had carried the last, and the first, Piper.

The walk was long, and a persistent, cold rain started to fall from the sky. The water pelted the back of her legs and dripped down her body. She felt the cold water on her scantily dressed body, and each drop awoke her senses.

Onnette raised her head and looked up at the passing trees, and although disoriented, she realized that she was being carried. She started to struggle and shift her weight. This disrupted Jacquemart's stride.

"Fucking bitch is waking up," he thought as he stopped and immediately threw her off his back and onto the ground.

Onnette hit the ground and tried to get up. Her muscles still partially paralyzed, she grabbed at the soil with her fingers, trying to pull herself away from him.

Jacquemart reached back into his pocket, and once again, removed the cattle prod. He stepped toward her and knelt down over her back.

She did not see the instrument, but felt the sense of impending harm.

He jabbed the gun into the back of her neck as his body held her down to the ground. There was no comparison between her weight and his, or his strength and hers.

The instrument buzzed and vibrated her body back into a catatonic state.

Jacquemart enjoyed the struggle. It was part of the hunt. He laughed as she passed out again. "You stupid bitch," he thought as he placed the instrument back into his pocket.

Jacquemart reached around and grabbed her by her ankles. The high-heeled shoes she was wearing interfered with his grip, so he ripped them off, breaking the strap and bruising her ankles. He reached down and picked up one of the shoes and threw it into the trees as far as he could throw. He turned and threw the other shoe in the other direction. He dragged her, face down, the rest of the way. He calculated the distance and had the goal of getting her to the timber shed.

With each step, he dragged Onnette's face along the dirt trail, bouncing over the rough terrain. The rough edges of broken tree branches and rocks formed hematomas on her cheeks, nose, and forehead. Her shirt rolled up and ripped, exposing her stomach to the same surface. The skin on her arms, legs, stomach, and face ripped open as her body bounced off the ground.

"I need to get to the timber shed," he said as he started to grow weary of the strenuous exercise.

Off in the distance, the small brown shed appeared.

With his energy restored, he maintained a quick pace until he reached the finish line, the timber shed.

He arrived at the door and let go of Onnette's ankles. He lifted her up as he squatted down to the ground. He struggled, as her body refused to co-operate. Her positioning was awkward, causing him to drop her. Her head fell forward and struck the boards of the shed; her cheek fell against the rough cut timbers that splintered the newly opened flesh of her face.

Jacquemart looked past her bleeding, purple, swollen skin. He stepped over her battered legs and torso to open the door to the shed. Once inside, he turned to drag her in, so he would not have to struggle with her, and laid her face down, neck in place, under the blade of his guillotine. He pulled the chair toward himself and sat it in front of her head. He left just enough distance to allow for his swift movement away from the imminent blade that was dangling above her the back of her neck.

Once again, he sat and waited patiently for her to wake up, not moving his eyes from her.

Once she started to stir, he picked up his foot and nudged at her body with his boot.

She moaned. She rolled to her side as she started gaining consciousness. The change in her position required Jacquemart to reposition her body back into its previous place. He let out a sigh, showing his annoyance, as he placed his boot on her shoulder and kicked her face back down.

She felt his boot and realized that she was still victim to the stranger. She cried out in pain as her nose struck the ground, "Pourquoi faites-vous cela (Why are you doing this?)"" she asked.

"Ta gueule! (Shut up)" he replied. "On your knees!"

Onnette was street smart enough to realize that she should go along with him if she had any chance of survival. She moved onto her knees, sat up, and tried to bring the large man sitting in front of her into focus. She was dizzy and her muscles were weak and shaking.

Jacquemart stood up and unzipped his pants. He pulled out his limp penis. He did not drop his pants, as he was already mentally three steps ahead. He did not want any errors when the blade dropped.

Onnette noticed that he had pulled out his penis. "I need to do this if I want to get out here," she thought. "I'll give him what he wants." She reached out with her hands to fondle his penis.

Jacquemart did not want to be fondled, but laughed at her desperation and entertained her action. "I'll move the slut into position once she sucks my dick," he thought.

Onnette noticed that the attacker was not hard. She stroked his limp penis without effect. She looked up at him, wondering what his problem was.

"Come on, big boy, calm down and let me please you."

Jacquemart reached down and grabbed her by her hair. "Do not speak to me, you filthy whore."

"Ah, okay, let go, let go," she yelled out.

He pulled her head by the hair into position. "Suck my cock!" he yelled at her. He was losing patience.

"Okay, okay," she replied. As she placed his limp penis in her mouth, Jacquemart looked away. He inadvertently looked onto the table where the letter lay. His mind was off into the distance.

The scene was now one step removed, as if he was watching a movie. He looked down and did not see a prostitute or his mother but his stepmother. She was giving oral sex to her lover. Jacquemart was off in the corner being forced to watch and learn the actions of his mother's profession. The actions being taught to the 10-year-old were intended to inflict mental damage.

"Watch my actions, Jacquemart, so you can see firsthand the actions of your whore mother." She would make him watch.

"Your mother spread her legs with dirty field workers, sweaty and lowly, for money, Jacquemart. Your father paid her to have you. You were a product, not a child of love, not a child conceived in wedlock," she would say on other occasions when she forced him to watch her on her back having sex.

Jacquemart jumped as he heard a knock on the door.

"Get out here, Jacquemart. Start dinner, now." He heard her yell through the closed door. "You pathetic little virgin, let go of your dick and get out here."

The deranged woman deeply despised the fact that his father did not give her a child, but she was forced to raise his bastard son. On his death bed, Adrian confessed that he had never loved her, that he had lived every day of his life in mourning over Odette.

"If you do not raise Jacquemart, you will live in squander, like the people you loathe," he threatened her in front of Jacquemart. Jacquemart dismissed the comment his father made about not loving his mother as a mere final act of vengeance toward her. His father could not have imagined the abuse she, in turn, inflicted upon Jacquemart as a result of his actions and confession.

"Come on, relax, baby," Onnette forced herself to say. She had experience in enticing men to orgasm. She knew if she had any chance of being free, it was essential for the abuser to have an orgasm.

She was also becoming agitated at the fact that Jacquemart was still not getting hard.

"He's not even paying attention to me. What do I do?" She became desperate and rubbed her breasts, faking a passionate moan while she continued to suck his penis. She rubbed the blood from her open cuts on her chest as it become sticky and smeared in circles around her nipples. Desperation drove her every move as she pretended she enjoyed it.

Jacquemart looked down and saw the blood, "It's time," he thought as he reached out and untied the rope.

Onnette saw his movement out of the corner of her eye and looked up. She caught an image of the blade seconds before it fell. She moved back out of sheer instinct.

The blade fell downward and sliced through the top of Onnette's scalp. She fell backwards and onto her butt. She looked up, revealing a heinous sight. Her forehead and nose had been cut off by the sharply honed blade. All that remained of her face was white frayed bits of cartilage and two nostril holes where her nose used to be. The skin of her forehead was gone, exposing the zig-zag patchwork of her skull. Her eyes were wide with her bone eye sockets exposed. The blade did not sever her head; it merely filleted her skin, hair, and nose from her head and face. In shock, she gazed forward at Jacquemart as a warm drop of liquid began to run down her chin.

"Water is dripping down my face," she thought. The horrific fact had not registered in her mind. The drop went into her eye, blurring her vision, covering the shed in a red haze. "Oh my god, it's blood!" She reached up to feel her nose, and instead, felt a flat surface. She raised her hand in front of her face, revealing her hand red. It was covered in her blood. She screamed a loud, unnerving cry of shock, horror and terror.

She looked to the ground and saw part of her skin lying in front of her.

"What have you done?" she screamed at Jacquemart.

CHAPTER EIGHTEEN
ONE STEP CLOSER TO HOME

Piper lifted her head from the pillow. "What was that?" She looked around. "Did I imagine it? Wait, there it is again."

She sat up and did not realize that the choke collar had been removed. She jumped out of bed and over to the window, in the direction of the sound. She looked down once she had realized that the collar and leash were gone. She reached up and felt her neck.

"The collar is gone. Oh my God, the collar is gone." She looked out the window, "Do I try to get out the window or try the door?"

She felt strength despite the fact that she had not eaten in days. She turned the iron latch and pushed the window open. She heard the scream again, this time louder. She looked out onto the roof of the timber shed.

The room that caged Piper was perched high within the rounded turret of the château that was connected to the roofless potion of the building by a long walkway. She looked down, disappointed to see that there was no window ledge, and the nearest roof was 20 feet below her and 90 degrees off the her room. She looked down to the ground below and assessed the distance to be more than 40 feet.

If not for her being pregnant, Piper may have risked climbing or jumping from the window, but she thought of her responsibility to the baby within her womb.

"I cannot get out of here from the window," she thought as she turned and ran for the door. She tried to turn the iron curved lever, but it was locked. The door was solid wood and seven feet high. She turned and ran to the bathroom that was adjacent to the bedroom. There was another window. She did not try it, as she realized that it would be the same. Her head snapped up and cocked to the right as she heard the scream again. She ran back to the window. Her eyes widened as she stared at the timber shed below.

"What have you done? Pourquoi? (Why)" Onnette leapt to her feet and tried to run for the door. Jacquemart grabbed her by her wrist and turned it until it snapped. She fell to her knees. He did not speak a word. He grabbed her by her forearm as her wrist dangled and flapped in the air. He dragged her back to a spot where the blade could finish the job. He leaned over, grabbed the rope, and pulled the blade back up to the ceiling.

He flipped Onnette onto her stomach; his penis was now hard and erect.

"On your knees," he commanded. "Suck me off if you want to live," he yelled loud enough to be heard over her crying and agonizing screams.

"I want to live," she cried as she opened her mouth to suck his penis. At this moment, all Onnette could think of was doing whatever it took to survive. Living was her only focus.

She placed her bloody lips around his hard penis. In Onnette's heart, she did not think she was going to live. However, she knew she did not have any chance of surviving if she did not do what he wanted. She did not have the spirit to suck his penis. Her lips quivered as she cried. She turned her head slightly and lifted her eyes. She saw the blade. Before she had time to move back again, Jacquemart let go of the rope.

This time, the blade cut her head from her neck, low, between her C4 and C5 vertebrae. Her body slumped as her left hand quivered for a second. Her bladder released, wetting the dried straw with urine.

There was blood pouring out of her jugular vein and into a puddle on the floor. The straw rug was soaked and stained red. Jacquemart stood in place and firmly gripped his penis. He rhythmically stroked it until he achieved his release.

His cum shot out onto her body as he moaned. His release was so powerful this time that he bit down on his bottom lip until it bled.

He felt every muscle in his body relax. For the first time since his last time, he had murdered; he was completely calm and satisfied. He looked at her body as if she were one of the dead boars or stags. She had always been just an animal to him, just another kill. He lifted his hand and wiped the blood from his lip. He looked down at the back of his hand and licked off the blood.

His thinking was clear; the voices stopped momentarily.

"Time to feed the boars," he said as he walked behind the body and pulled it back by the ankle. He walked back over to where her head lay and kicked back the blood soaked mat. He walked over to her head and kicked it into the newly dug hole. With eyes still looking upward, her head slid across the ground and fell into the hole. He kicked the mat back over the top of the hole as a means of preliminary concealment, until he could return to fill it in.

He walked over to the door and opened it. He picked up her ankle and started to drag her body. He noticed that he was leaving a trail of blood behind him.

"The rain will wash it away." He continued to drag her out the door and around the side of the shed to his truck.

Piper saw Jacquemart leave the shed. She also saw the body of Onnette as he dragged her to the truck. Jacquemart looked up out of sheer instinct and saw Piper looking at him through the turret window. He looked her in the eyes. She looked at him. She did not run this time. She could not. She was frozen. She felt as if she was watching a movie rather than actually seeing firsthand the after effects of murder. Since being abducted, Piper had remained confused. She had fear for her life, and then her abductor took care of her, instilling safety in her. Now, after seeing this horrific sight, she was numb and detached.

"He could not have murdered her," Piper thought.

"He has never laid a hand on me; in fact, he has fed and bathed me." She felt confused and conflicted. She could not pull herself away from the window.

"D'une minute," he called out. She looked at him, puzzled. "I must be late for her dinner," he said to himself. His short respite from the delusions had ended. Piper, looking out the window, was not the strange American; she was his stepmother watching his moves, as she always did.

"He said just one minute?" Nico has used that phrase. "I know what that means." She asked herself then, "Wait for what?" An intense jab of fear struck her consciousness and awoke her to reality. "Am I next?" She quickly turned away and walked back to the bed, "I will survive this," she repeated to herself. She sat on the bed and looked down at her stomach with feelings of fear and confusion.

Piper sat and thought about what she had just witnessed.

"Was she actually headless?" she questioned herself. "She was again dressed like a prostitute. I wonder if he has something against prostitutes." She thought about the park where she was abducted. "There were women standing around, now that I remember it. Was it some sort of brothel?" She looked around the room at the elaborate setting.

"He thought I was a whore." She started to put the pieces together as Jacquemart threw his victim into the back of the truck.

He casually walked over to the driver side, opened the door, got in, and started the engine. He drove the truck to the side of the château. Piper could not see where he was driving.

When Jacquemart reached the boar kennels, he walked into the butcher room and methodically and robotically severed Onnette's arms and legs. Rigor mortis had not yet set in. Her body was still moveable to the saw's sharp blade.

The boars had not been fed since the last body. They ran in circles, snorting, hoofing the ground, and growling at each other when they got too close to each one's space. Hungry and territorial for food, once he threw in on leg, then the other, then an arm, and the other, they devoured her flesh, muscle, bone, nails, and left only torn bloody clothes, which they trampled into the muddy ground.

"I must make her dinner. I am sure she is hungry." He picked up his pace, "I must hurry."

He was functioning back within the confines of his state of mass confusion and delusions.

CHAPTER NINETEEN
NOTHING TO DECLARE

François, staring at the swirling liquid as he stirred his cafe au lait slowly, stalling, mumbled, "I am not in the mood to be here today."

He walked over to the large, round table at the entrance to the lobby and rearranged the flowers in the tall, slim vase. He then picked up the newspapers that were neatly folded into three and restacked them. As he held them up together and tapped them down on the table, he glanced at the first newspaper headlines.

"Touriste Piege (tourist trap)." This caught François' attention. He opened the paper and began to read, "Local police fear local prostitute and American tourist have been abducted."

He read the entire article and looked up. "This is Mrs. Blanche. I must tell Georgess." He walked briskly into the back office where the manager sat behind the neatly arranged desk.

"Monsieur," he paused politely waiting for a response to indicate whether he could continue his interruption.

"What is it, François?" The manager spoke to him without looking up as he continued to write.

"You need to see this." He held out the paper.

"François, bring it to me. You can see that I am very busy. And return to the front desk, please." He was brief and curt.

The young man walked over and set the paper down on the desk in front of his boss and walked back to the front desk, closing the glass door behind him.

The manager read the article with an overwhelming sense of presentiment. "François," he screamed out, "Come here, tout de suite."

François stayed close to the office. He knew the news would alarm the manager. He turned and quickly walked into the office, closing the door behind him.

"Yes, Monsieur," he replied.

"This article is about Mrs. Blanche. Did you know the police were here questioning Mr. Blanche?" he asked with great exasperation.

"No, sir, I understand that they came in the evening after my shift was over," he replied quietly.

"And how did you know this? I just asked you if you were aware that the police were here, so obviously, you knew; how?" The manager's anger grew with every thought.

"Monique was on desk duty that night; she told me." François knew he had breached protocol in neglecting to inform the manager. "I told her to inform you," he concluded in an attempt to restore his dismissive actions.

"Well, she did not. I expected you would have told me. You are head of the front desk. I am noting this in your personnel file. Is Mr. Blanche in?" he asked.

"I don't know, Monsieur," he replied before continuing, "Should I call the room?""No, accompany me to the room. Call Stephan to watch the desk." The manager pushed the chair back, stood up, and handed the paper to the uneasy young man, "Throw this away."

He pushed past François and strode out of the office and into the lobby. François shadowed his every move silently, throwing the paper in the garbage behind the desk as he walked past.

The two employees of Courcilles Hotel walked quietly and quickly down the gravel paths to the room occupied by Nico and Nicole. The manager knocked with force on the wooden door.

"Mr. Blanche, this is the manager; please open the door."

Nicole slowly got out of the bed, carrying the glass of champagne she was drinking. She did not bother to put a robe over her bra and thong. She opened the door two feet, which was enough room to expose her garb.

"Excusez-moi, madame, is Monsieur Blanche in?" the manager asked as he looked down with professionalism. François stared directly at Nicole's French cut bra that pushed up her saline breasts.

"No, he is not." She stopped and starred at the manager, then at the young Frenchman who was still staring at her breasts.

Georges replied calmly, without alarm, "Can you please provide me with the number to his cell phone. It is very important that I contact him. François, take the number down."

Nicole replied, "318-908-0000," then shut the door. "Fucking assholes," she said loud enough for him to hear as she walked back to the bed, gulping down a full glass of champagne.

The manager pulled out his cell phone and dialed the number without asking François to repeat it. He walked down the path to the office, waiting for Nico to answer the phone.

"Qui?" Nico asked as he answered his phone from the kitchen of the restaurant he was working in.

"Mr. Blanche, this is the hotel manager. It is imperative that you to return to the hotel immediately." He was cordial but stern.

"I don't have time for this. What is it?" Nico replied as he shook the sauté pan, flipping the chanterelles high into the air. "Haven't I been disturbed enough already?" Nico spoke while cradling his cell phone between his ear and shoulder, while continuing to work at the cook top. Nico was brilliant at multitasking while in the kitchen. "Non, do not incorporate the demi glace yet!" he yelled out to one of the young chefs who was assisting him. "Marco, come here and take this pan away from this monkey."

Marco had just arrived in France as Chef Blanche's sous chef. He hurried over and grabbed the pan from the chef without speaking to him. He glanced at him as if to imply that he was sorry. Marco knew how it felt to be belittled by the chef.

"I will not keep you, Monsieur Blanche. I would rather not speak about the incident over the phone. At your earliest convenience, please come to the hotel. When you arrive, please come to the front desk and ask for me. Thank you." He hung up the phone without waiting for a response from Nico.

Georges immediately called for his assistant, "François, when Monsieur Blanche arrives, please send him to my office."

Nico called out for his assistant, ironically, at the same time, "Take this phone from my shoulder and hang it up."

Nico continued to work in the kitchen until the meal he was preparing for the celebrity chefs' benefit was prepped.

"Marco, I have to step out for an hour. Please see to it that the vegetables are not over-processed, pureed will make the night a fucking nightmare." He walked out of the kitchen as he untied his apron and laid it on the main counter.

He had only been in France for three days. He had not relaxed nor spent any time with Nicole. His mind drifted to Piper. "I wonder what I will find when I get back to the States."

Nico was fairly certain that Piper must have left France. He was also certain that she would not speak to him if he attempted to contact her, so he did not. He drove back to the hotel and entered the lobby, still in his chef's whites.

"Good afternoon, Monsieur Blanche," François greeted him. "Let me call Monsieur Turgan for you."

François walked back to the manager's office. "Excusez-moi, Monsieur, Monsieur Blanche is here to speak with you."

"Send him in," Georges replied.

François walked back out of the office. "Monsieur Blanche, please follow me." He escorted Nico to the back office. Once inside, he walked out and closed the door.

"Please, sit down, Monsieur Blanche," Georges urged Nico.

"We need to make this short, so I would rather not. What was so important that you required my personal appearance?" Nico was clearly perturbed.

"Well, Monsieur Blanche, we seem to have a problem," Georges began. "Have the police named you as a suspect in your wife's disappearance?"

"You insult me, and I do not have time for this." Nico did not answer the question; he turned and reached for the door knob.

"Monsieur Blanche, I feel it in the best interest of all parties if you and Ms. Nicole leave the hotel. I can suggest another one if you would like," Georgess spoke quickly so as to get through to Nico before he left the office.

Nico turned around with a look of dismay. "I will not leave this hotel. I have two more nights booked, and I do not have time for this. I am sure you are aware that I am cooking at the celebrity chefs' benefit at L'Orange tonight and tomorrow."

"I am very sorry, but I must insist that you find another hotel." Georges stood up and called for François.

François appeared within seconds, opening the door into Nico's back.

"My apologies, Monsieur Blanche," he said in embarrassment.

The manager had fully expected the response that Nico delivered. He had already directed his assistant to call other hotels in the area and arrange alternative accommodations for him.

"Were you able to find Monsieur Blanche another hotel?" he asked.

François replied, "Yes, I have booked him at Hotel du Chassey."

Nico did not speak. He merely stood with his back to François, who stood just outside the room with his arms folded over his chest.

"Do you realize who I am? What bad relations I will cause here?" Nico yelled at the manager.

Georges opened his mouth to reply, but before he could speak, Nico continued just as the moment he opened his mouth.

"Save your petty, ignorant, banal rambling for some two-bit American or German tourist. I am not a tourist; I am Nico Blanche. I graced your petty hotel. I chose to leave it; do you understand that? I am leaving by my choice and not yours, so do not speak personally to me any further." Nico spoke as if the manager was one of his commi chefs.

Nico turned and walked out, pushing François out of the way. As François fell backward, Nico replied, "Out of my way, you little squandering mouse."

"Follow him and see that they both leave," Georges said as Nico left his office. He gestured quickly with his hand for him to catch up with Nico.

"And don't speak to him, François. We do not need a scene here," he added.

Georges sat back and thought about the missing American. He felt he had played some part in this, due to the fact that she went missing immediately upon leaving the hotel. He sat back in his chair and just stared at the open door.

François stepped quickly, scurrying behind Nico, following him out the lobby and down the path to the room with his head down.

Nico did not turn around to acknowledge him, although he could hear François breathing slightly as he jogged behind Nico's large, thunderous strides.

He arrived at the room and reached into his pocket for the key, quickly realizing that it was not in his chef's pants. He stopped and looked down, remembering that the key was in his pants pocket back at the restaurant.

"Putain de merde!" Nico screamed out.

François kept his head down, hoping to stay out of Nico's line of fire.

Nico reached out to the door and beat on it firmly several times. "Nicole, open up, now!" He was demanding and discourteous.

The door opened and Nicole greeted him, dressed in jeans, a tee shirt, and red high-heeled Louboutin shoes that Nico had purchased for her prior to the trip.

"Hello," she was surprised and elated to see him, as most of her stay had been spent alone.

"Pack your things; we are leaving," he commanded.

"Why?" she asked in a high-pitched whine.

"We are being asked to leave by the management," Nico replied as he stood in the room, expecting her to pack both his and her clothes and personal items.

Nicole grabbed the suitcase and slung it onto the bed. "Is this because of your bitch wife?"

"Just pack, Nicole," Nico replied without addressing her question.

Once all of the items were packed, Nico turned and walked out of the room ahead of Nicole. She struggled to get her suitcase off the bed. She walked, taking inch-long steps, leaning over the opposite side of the bag for balance.

François noticed her struggling and spoke up, "Madame, allow me to assist you." He took the bag from her hand and carried it out, setting it outside the door. He walked back in and picked up the other suitcase and did the same.

"I will call for the bellman," he said to Nico as he started to walk down the path to the car.

"Nicole, hurry up, I have to get back to the restaurant," he called out as she tried to catch up with him, running in her six-inch heels.

She called out to him, devoid of the reality of the petulance that Nico was feeling, "What are you making, by the way?"

Nico did not break stride. He rolled his eyes and yelled back to her without turning his head to address her, "Blancs de Rouget au Pistou de Legumes et Fumet de Vin Rouge."

He was fully aware that she did not speak French and would not have a remote clue what the meal was.

"Will you bring me a doggie bag?" she asked with 100% sincerity.

Nico replied, "We are not in Pennsylvania anymore, Darling. I don't have time for your inane banter. Post Haste."

Nicole thought to herself, "I bet Piper is having more fun that I am, wherever she is."

CHAPTER TWENTY
LOIN OF STAG WITH POIVRADE

The white ice crystals on the sides of the freezer changed to red and melted as Jacquemart shuffled through the meat in the freezer, looking for stag loins.

"I can defrost the meat in cold water while I prepare the pommes fondants (potato)..." His mind raced through a menu that he could make easily based on his repertoire.

His hands were covered in dried blood and the red color of the new blood turned maroon. Underneath, his short nails were black with encrusted blood. He did not notice; he did not wash his hands. Jacquemart was focused on the meal that he was late in preparing.

He walked down the stone steps and into the dusty wine cellar. He walked to the back wall where the displayed bottles lacked dust. He looked at the foil at the end of the bottle, knowing each wine by heart. He pulled out a bottle and ascended the steps.

Once the meal was cooked and the plate prepared, he methodically and meticulously set the tray with white linens, crystal, and bone china. He placed two small silver salt and pepper shakers on the tray, and as the final touch, a crystal finger bowl. His stepmother required the finger bowl anytime she ate red meat.

Jacquemart looked up at the clock and realized her dinner was 37 minutes late.

He rushed the tray through the hall and up the stairs, trying to maintain perfect balance. He reached the hall and set the tray on the ground while he searched for the right key.

Piper heard the keys in the hall and ran back to the bed out of habit. She sat where the linens had the indent of her body.

Jacquemart entered, and Piper could not believe what she saw. He was covered in blood. His clothes were soaked. His hands showed little clean skin. His unemotional face had splashes of blood from one side to the other. He was detached and vacuous.

Piper did not speak. She watched the grotesque figure as it approached carrying a crisp, white tray that was visually disturbed by red finger prints everywhere he touched the fabric to set it in place.

Jacquemart concentrated on the tray. He walked over to the bed and set the tray on the ground. He lifted the napkin and shook it out before placing it on Piper's lap.

As his hands reached toward her, she sucked in the air around her and held her breath. She was muted out of shock and fear. She did move a muscle. Her eyes did not move, nor did she blink. Piper acquiesced Jacquemart to go through the strange ceremony without disturbance.

She was starving. She smelled the meat and potatoes. She had not eaten in days. Going from starvation to heavy gourmet meals was in its own form, tortuous, but she knew she had to eat for her and her baby.

Jacquemart set the tray on her lap. She reached out from sheer hunger to grab the piece of meat. Jacquemart grabbed her hand before it reached the tray. He placed a strong, painful grip on her wrist. He did not look at her. He held her wrist tightly. Piper's every muscle felt the pulsating nerve rush from sheer panic; she did not move. Once he freed her wrist, she pulled it to her stomach and held it with her other hand. Still, she did not look at him.

Jacquemart continued to go through the motions. He quickly refocused and dismissed her actions and his reaction. He reached behind his waist and removed a cork screw from his back pocket and opened the end, revealing the sharp metal end. He looked at it.

"Should I stab her in the neck?" he thought. "Her lover is probably in the closet, hiding this time, because my father is in the woods. She is a lying whore."

He looked up and stared at Piper. He saw his stepmother.

Piper held her breath once again, "Is he going to stab me with that?" she asked herself as she made the decision to stay perfectly still.

He turned and looked at the bottle of Fortant de France, Cabernet Sauvignon, and picked it up. He slowly and methodically uncorked the bottle perfectly and handed Piper the cork, his eyes fixed on the ground.

Piper thought, "What do I do with this? Do I smell it?" She reached out and accepted the cork. "This is so strange. If I don't, what will he do?" Piper smelled the cork, holding true to the surreal ceremony. She spoke for the first time in a calm and quiet voice, "It is acceptable." She felt like she was acting in a movie and convinced herself it was her only opportunity to survive. Piper remembered playing house and serving toast and jelly to her father while he read in his library. She began to live in this one person removed state.

Jacquemart did not acknowledge Piper. He poured a small amount of red wine into the crystal wine glass and handed it to her.

"I will smell and then taste the wine," she thought as she accepted the glass from him.

Piper could not remember the last time she had had water. She did not stop to consider the effect that wine would have on her baby, as it had not had water either. Out of dire thirst and primary instinct, she grabbed the glass, and despite what she had planned in her mind, she did not smell, sip from, or swirl the glass. She held it to her mouth and gulped the wine. She felt a sharp edge cut into her lip. She quickly removed the glass, put her finger to her bottom lip, pulled it away, and looked at it. She had cut her mouth on a broken edge of the glass.

She looked over at Jacquemart, who quickly turned his shoulder away as a pavlovian dog moving away from over-conditioning. He stepped back and held his arm up to block his face.

"It's okay, it was nothing," Piper said quickly and quietly out of apathy. She felt his fear and did not want to enrage or incite him.

Jacquemart squared his shoulders back up and looked at her. His eyes appeared dark and endless. He did not respond; he just looked at her for the first time, seeing her as a human with human characteristics and emotions, just like him.

As he looked at her, Piper felt a sharp, stabbing pain in her abdomen. "Oh," she said as she slumped forward, placing her hands on her stomach.

She had not experienced this pain before. She was concerned for her baby. Piper looked at Jacquemart and said, "Bébé." The stabbing pain struck her again and her focus shifted back to her developing child. She was not comfortable telling her capture of her condition. She spoke extemporaneously. Her focus remained on her child, instead of Jacquemart's reaction or next move.

Jacquemart was bewildered. He watched her wince in pain. "She is pregnant?" He was filled with disgust toward himself. The thought of himself trying to entice a pregnant woman in some confusing way affronted him. "She was protecting her child. She refused to have ungodly acts with me," he thought as he watched her. "She is undefiled. She protected her baby."

Jacquemart left the tray, turned, and walked quickly away, closing the door behind him. He walked a few steps, realizing that he did not lock the door. He turned and pulled out his keys and locked the door. This time, he ran down the hall.

"She has a baby in her? I have captured and placed her in a cage, and she has a child in her. I have caused her baby to live as I did, captured."

He ran into the kitchen and out of the house. He stood and looked out into the evening sky that loomed over the tree line, encouraging moodiness.

"What have I done?" he thought as he condemned his actions. He ran down the path, beaten down with overuse. He reached his utopia. He saw his maternal structure that offered him comfort and peace. He kicked open the door to the timber shed, entered, and slammed the door shut.

He reached down and peeled back the carpet, exposing the two newly covered holes. He fell to his knees and dug at the soil with his fingertips.

He exposed the first victim. He looked down and saw the closed eyes of the dark skinned woman, wyes closed, soil muddied into all the crevices that poured or seeped blood.

He turned and moved his body on the ground as he crawled to the next hole. He uncovered it to expose the woman who he imagined looked like his mother, Odette.

Her eyes were open, looking upward. She looked angelic and pure. Her skin was purple around the eyes. Her grey eyes were fixed to the heavens, as if she was speaking to God.

"I forced her to be unpure." He turned his condemning attitude toward one of compassion. He looked over and searched for the letter.

He stood up, sobbing, and picked up the letter. He reread the intense words within the confines of his mind until he reached part of the letter that read, "My angelic Odette, you were sent to release me, though fleeting. My heart flew free and soared above, looking down on a pathetic existence; But rejoice, for I am finally free. In Perpetum, Adrian."

He fell back and curled into the fetal position. He wrapped his hands around his body and held himself. Jacquemart had never been embraced or held by anyone at any point in his life.

His father was too angry to show emotion, his stepmother, too spiteful to mother him at any stage, and most importantly, his birth mother was the one who had tried to kill him at birth. From the time he was removed from his mother's jail cell, the only compassion he received was from the guard who intervened and rescued him from drowning in the toilet.

He did not remember nor feel that moment.

"God, why do you punish me? I was born a prisoner, like my father. I am a prisoner of this mind, and body, and place."

He cried as he thought the harsh words of veracity.

"My dogs… CeCeine will comfort me and show me love." He jumped up without lucidity. He did not recall that CeCeine was dead, by his hand.

The death was adding up: his mother, father, CeCeine, the boars, the stags, the two prostitutes. He thought about those who had died by his hand, and those who had died after a life deprived of joy.

He ran out of the timber shed and through the woods, the light of day now denying him clear focus.

He ran, into brush, this time; low branches reached out and slapped his face, exposing his blood. His blood now mixed with Onnette's dried blood, ironically.

He reached his home, which now appeared dead. He stopped and stood, looking up. He saw the château as a decayed tombstone in an abandoned cemetery.

The stone was the same grayish white shade, darkened buy age. He ran around the house. He reached the dog kennels. The pack was hungry. Deprived of food for days, they barked, bit one another, and jumped over each other, trampling one another until the weakest dog was pounded to the ground.

He walked into the pen and called out, "CeCeine, come, girl!" She did not run to him as usual.

"CeCeine!" he called louder in a panicked tone.

He stood and waited. The strongest of the pack made his way to Jacquemart and jumped on his legs as they all barked and jumped for his attention.

CeCeine never came. The crippling, debilitating truth struck him. Reality collided with his delusional world.

"I stabbed her. I killed my beloved CeCeine." He fell to his knees and cried with his head in his hands. One of CeCeine's pups bounded over to him and licked his face. He looked up at the white, brown, and black patched dog. He grabbed it and pulled it to his chest.

"What have I done?" He hugged the puppy until it struggled to be free, its energy fuelled by excitement.

Jacquemart stood up. He walked out of the pen and over to the feed barrels. He pushed off the wooden top and filled up the bowls that lay in the barrels. He took the bowls into the kennel and placed them in various locations.

"I will feed you. You should not suffer," he said to them as he placed the bowls on the ground. His mind shifted back to Piper.

"She has tried to protect her baby. She has not had impure acts with me." He went through the motions of feeding the dogs without paying attention to them. His mind still fixated on Piper and her baby. "She was sent to me. She was sent to release me. I have caused her to live the way I have spent all my life resenting."

He stood up and walked out, latching the gate as he exited the cage. He suddenly stopped and turned around and looked at them, then at the cage, then up toward Piper's room.

"I have caged everything I care about. I see this; they should be free. They should not be imprisoned." He reached out and unlatched the kennel door.

"They deserve freedom and I have starved them from it." He turned and walked back on his course without opening the kennel door.

He reached the boar kennels. He stood and watched the beastly animals as they ran around the pen, waiting for their next meal. Their hooves kicked and pierced one another as they fought to the front of the pen.

Jacquemart stood and watched the unruly pandemonium. He looked to the ground, darkness concealing the black, course, bristled beasts. Through the veil of darkness, peeking through the mud and fecal matter was a yellow piece of fabric.

He became fixated on the material remains of his last victim.

"I forced it on her. What if she was with child? That child felt the pain. Did her child feel pain?" His mind raced onwards, as did his self-condemnation. He could not think of anything other than the three women; he imagined them all carrying children, all carrying males. He assimilated these imaginary male fetuses into himself.

"I cannot live knowing that I have done this—the imprisonment and pain?"

He ran out of the pen, leaving it open. The boars, one by one, ran out and away from their death sentence. They ran into the woods as fast as their legs would permit.

Jacquemart walked, this time, back toward the house. He was confused, crying, chastising himself, and falling back into delirium.

"I am proud, Dad. The hounds listen to me," he said into the night air.

"That is good, Jacquemart. One day, you will have this. Take care of the hounds. The dogs will be your closest friends and quietest advisors." Jacquemart heard his father's words resonate in his head.

"I let you down, Dad." He stopped and looked up at Piper's room. He had an epiphany. "Her unborn son will be you; take care of the things and ones you love, Son," Jacquemart spoke as his father would have spoken.

"She will raise her son as I should have been raised. He will take care of the hounds as I should have." He looked into the dark room; moments of flickering light came from the one candle he had left in the room.

"I wonder if she is hungry, or thirsty." When he had delivered Piper's food, he was in his delusional state. He was serving his stepmother, and she did not want water, ever.

"The American with child needs water." He raced into the house. He grabbed a white antique porcelain water pitcher, filled it with water, and picked up a glass.

He walked through the halls hoping she was not dead, each step taken with trepidation.

He reached the room and grabbed the keys. He opened the door. Piper was sitting on the bed with the food tray still on her lap.

He walked over to her. The plate was clean. He looked at her; she was leaning back onto the pillows. He smelled the overwhelming smell of vomit. He looked around her body and saw the red meat and sauce thrown up on the bed. He picked up the tray and set it on the floor. He poured the water into the glass and set the pitcher down. He reached over pulled her forward, cradling her. Her head fell back. He sat on the bed and moved his hand up to her neck. He allowed a small amount of water to fall into her mouth. He did this several times.

When he fed Piper half of the glass of water, he walked into the bathroom and grabbed a towel. He placed it under the tap and rung it out in cold water.

He walked back to Piper and wiped her face. Her skin was white and her clothes, dirty and sweaty. He stood up and walked over to the dresser and pulled out a white linen gown that was faded and musty. He walked back over to the bed and held Piper up, took off her shirt, and turned his head when her bra was exposed.

He lifted her up enough to pull the linen gown over her head and down over her body. Only then did he remove her jeans.

He folded her soiled clothes that displayed her struggle and set them on the dresser. He pulled her down, laying her on the bed with her head on the pillow.

He looked at her stomach and thought to himself, "Protegez l'innocent (Protect the innocent)."

He lifted her arm and placed his hand softly on her stomach, "Le vôtre héritera la terre (Yours will inherit the earth)."

He turned and walked out of the room. He paused at the door once he stood outside of the bedroom. He turned and looked back at Piper before closing the door. She lay still, dressed in the long faded yellow linen night gown. She looked like she was from a painting in a different era. She rested quietly with her head on the pillow.

He recalled his father's letter to his mother and spoke out to her softly, with heartfelt emotion. Piper was the only person in his lifetime who he had spoken to from his heart, devoid of anger and hatred.

"My angelic Odette, you were sent to release me."

He whispered again the words from his father's hand. He turned and closed the door, closing the barrier between him and her.

"I will lock this door for the last time," he thought as he reached into his pocket, and without conviction, locked Piper, once again, inside the bedroom, imprisoning her.

CHAPTER TWENTY-ONE
A NEW DAY

Piper woke up feeling better for the first time since setting foot in France. The sun peeked through the window, fortifying her soul with hope.

She sat up, realizing that she was sleeping on her back.

"I never sleep on my back," she thought as she sat up. She looked down and noticed the linen gown on her body. She reached down and grabbed a portion of the fabric and lifted it up to view it.

"I don't remember putting this on. I have no idea where this came from."

She looked around the room. Her tee shirt and jeans were folded and placed neatly on the dresser. She noticed the tray from the night before and her memory flooded back, "He brought me a tray of venison. The wine? My lip?" She reached up and felt her bottom lip that was now scabbed over. "He must have fed me and then dressed me." She reached to see if she had on her bra and underwear.

"God, no, please, did he rape me?" she said as she felt for her bra strap and reached down and felt her underwear in a panic. She let out a sigh of relief, followed by an intense stare into the room that imprisoned her.

"What is this all about?" Piper thought. She could not place all the pieces of the stranger's actions together such that the events made sense.

"If he had wanted to kill me, he would have. Now, he's taking care of me?" She did not recall the scene she witnessed of the dead woman.

She got out of bed and walked to the door. It was locked. She hit her forehead on the solid wood frame and pounded her fists against the austere structure in frustration.

"NO, NO, NO. I want out of here." She began to scream, "Let me out, please, let me out! Please!"

She paused with her ear to the door, waiting to hear the keys, footsteps, or any sign of her captor.

She waited for 30-40 minutes perched at the door, beating it and screaming.

"He is not coming," she thought. She turned and walked to the window.

The day was bright. The grounds appeared regal, even in their state of disrepair.

She reached up and struggled briefly with the ornate iron latch. She pushed both long paned windows open and stretched her head out.

Piper thought she saw a dog. She looked again and saw a pack of dogs, "Those look like beagles," She thought as she looked ahead, watching them.

The dogs jumped and circled one another. Then they ran in a full on sprint to the woods, but they would turn and run back, never going past the tree line.

"They must be trained; they are obviously his. He can't be a total monster if he has dogs." She tried to analyze her captor, but could not. He was a total dichotomy.

"He must have a human side," she thought as she watched the pack.

She tried to count how many hounds there were, "... 15, 16, 17..." Piper counted up to 30 dogs. "They look as if they don't get out enough," she said as she watched them play with each other as a group, enraptured with their newfound freedom.

Her eyes scanned the grounds for her captor once again, but he could not be found.

Piper noticed a long, still reflecting pond on the far end of the property. She saw a statue for the first time. It was of a woman standing, looking down over her shoulder in perfect, simple elegance. The statue stood five or so feet high. Her silhouette, perfectly reflected in the water, blurred only when the breeze rippled it.

Piper now stood in awe of the grounds that she was discovering. The locked door to her cell, at this minute, did not exist.

She pushed her head further out the window until her balance was compromised. She turned her body and looked in the opposite direction. She could see a small village down the slope of the property, in the valley. Another large château stood in the center of the town.

"The village is perfect. Look at all the small slate roofed houses," she said to herself. "That château is not nearly as large as this one," she thought, not designating Jacquemart's château as a prison.

Piper stood in shock of her reaction, "I speak as if I am the lady of the house."

She felt a warm glow of pride overwhelm her. Her eyes teared up and her arms were clustered with goose bumps. Although the château was not hers, and it, in reality imprisoned her, at this moment in time, it did not matter to her. She embraced Jacquemart's château. This was something that had not been done in decades.

Piper could see the span of the château for the first time. The L-shaped building looked almost like a castle to her. She was in the turret, but she could also see a tower structure the same height as the rounded building she was in. It did not have a roof, however.

"This man has great stature," she thought as she surveyed the neighboring homes and châteaux. "This château is the largest and the most beautiful."

Her mind shifted to her captor. "Why has he let it fall into such disrepair?" She wondered about his financial situation, "He must not be able to afford it. How sad," she said. She now felt great sorrow for the man who had captured her and killed prostitutes, but cared for, fed, and bathed her.

The grass valley was verdant and emerald green. Grape vineyards were scattered amongst the hills, trees, and châteaux.

Piper thought through the archives of her memory.

"I have had the most horrific experience; I have been treated violently; I have been imprisoned; I have been taken care of; and I have been fed, bathed, and clothed." She started to go deeper into her memory of the recent events that impacted and embraced her entire being.

Piper recalled her father and mother, how they had raised her to be loving and forgiving. Piper remembered that she relived memories of her and father that she had not recalled in years.

"I remembered Nico when he loved me. I felt his embrace when we both embraced each other. I loved him with every fiber of my being. I will not let go of that. I will not discard those memories."

Piper allowed herself to cry openly as she thought.

"This child will know Nico—the Nico that was confident and loving, when he was thoughtful and we were inseparable." She looked out at the tree line.

"This child will know my father and mother. It will know how to respect nature and history." She recalled her father's library and all of the books she was left after his death—the books she had read as a child about Europe, American history, and poetry.

Piper moved away from the window and walked back to the bed. She walked past it for the first time, to the dresser where the large mirror hung.

She looked at herself, past her physical appearance. For the first time in her life, she saw who she really was.

"I don't need Nico. I can stand on my own, by the strength of my skills." She saw a confident chef.

Piper continued to look into the mirror, deeper.

"I deserve to be treated the way my father treated my mother, like a queen. This is what he wanted for me. This stranger has treated me more respectfully than my husband has." She saw a beautiful, caring, compassionate woman.

"My child deserves to see France, in all its beauty, with humility." She saw an honest, humble, hard-working woman— the person her parents had raised her to be.

She once again remembered her father, the strong, silent force in her life.

"I want you to be proud of me," she thought as envisioned her father's embracing eyes. "You would not be proud of how my husband has treated me."

Piper turned away from the mirror and paced the room. She walked toward the painting that watched over her. She walked toward the bathroom. She looked at all the places she could not reach when she was chained to the bed. She noticed porcelain, hand-painted vases, and a silver mirror and brush sets.

She wondered who lived in the grand room.

"Oh my God, the letter." She panicked and ran to the bed, lifting up the pillow. It was not there. "Where did the letter go?" She pulled back the covers and threw the pillows onto the floor frantically. She fell to her knees and looked under the high framed bed.

The letter was not in the room. She sat back and folded her legs, "I should've given the letter to him." Piper felt as if she had let him down in some way. Once again, she began to cry openly.

Piper was filled with emotions—emotions she could not contain.

She stood up and began to pace the room once again.

She thought of her captor. "He must have been abused. He is deeply disturbed and tormented. It is strange, but I feel sorry for him." She allowed herself to emote about his psychological state until she felt a sudden cramping in her stomach.

"How am I going to get out of here?" she thought. She heard stones crushing together. She jumped up and ran to the open window. She looked out to see the back of a large, mysterious man, walking with his head down, arms hanging low to his sides. "He is going back to that shed," she thought as she watched him.

"Please, no more killing."

She wondered to herself, "Should I call out to him?" Piper was conflicted and bereft. She could not speak, although she wanted to. She just watched silently, trying to plot her best move.

Jacquemart walked into the timber shed and closed the door.

Piper could not see into the small wooden structure. She stood at the window and wondered, "What is he doing? What will I see next?" She could not remove her eyes from the shed, although she wanted to. Her eyes were fixed on the shed due to a curious magnetic pull.

Piper was worried about her captor.

CHAPTER TWENTY-TWO
MY GIFT TO YOU

Jacquemart knew the sequence of his next steps. He walked out of the shed after organizing his thoughts. He got into his truck and drove to the back of the house. As he drove, the hounds chased his truck, barking and running to catch up to it. He looked in his rear view mirror and watched briefly as they ran after it. He pulled back to the kennel to place out feed bins.

"I don't know when they will eat again." He watched them as they ran over to the bins and gathered around the many bowls. "They no longer bite and crawl over one another to get their feed," he thought, amazed at how much calmer and happier they seemed as a group.

He opened the door and walked through the house, some of the dogs following him, slipping on the stone surface, claws screeching as they slid. This was the first time any dog other than CeCeine had been in the house.

He paused in the kitchen briefly to pick up the house phone. He dialed a number, paused, and left voicemail. After a minute of speaking, he set the receiver back down on the antiquated stand and proceeded through the house.

He walked into a sitting room at the back of the house. Mounted wild boar, stag, and hare set the tone of stillness and death in the room. He walked to the back of the room and up to a large safe. He knelt down and turned the worn brass dial until the door clicked open. He pulled out a metal box and shoved it under his arm. He left the door open and walked to the ornate table that displayed several decanters and a cognac bottle. He opened the bottle that proudly displayed a large Dartmount crest in the middle. He reached over and grabbed a crystal ballooned cognac glass. He poured a tall glass of valuable cognac that was produced under the family name. He lifted the glass to his lips and smelled the liquor. He closed his eyes and allowed the sharp smell to awaken his senses. He slowly drank a sip of the cognac and allowed the flavor to rest on his tongue before swallowing.

He drank the glass slowly, imbibing and embellishing the ritual as his father had taught him. He set the glass down and left the room without turning back.

He walked back to his truck and backtracked to the timber shed. He paused before opening the door and looked up to the window of Piper's room. He hoped to have one last look at his redeemer.

She was not there. He imagined her lying in the bed sleeping peacefully.

He walked through the door and sat at the table. He placed the metal box down and opened it. He pulled out a pen and the official Dartmount stationery that was used to authenticate documents.

Jacquemart sat at the table, looking down at the blank page of thick linen paper. He looked over at his father's love that had been written on the same stationery, printed by the same local printer for hundreds of years.

He struggled to extract the words from his mind and place them on paper. He knew what he wanted to say, but had never written such a letter.

He wanted his words to show his contriteness. He needed the words to release him cathartically. Most importantly, he longed for the American to understand.

He began to write in French,

My Angel of Chance,

I have lived the life I was given the best that I could. I have learned more from you in the last few days than I have the whole of my existence. The letter you found was a gift sent by God and channeled through you to awaken me from this stoic state of vacuity.

I have been swimming against a large wave of ire and rage. I am effete and motionless now. I was conceived through love.

I was poisoned by hatred.

It was the prejudice of stature and ignorance of emotion that caused my birth in captivity. Desperation and stature separated me from being. I cannot write of love, hope, or dreams, as I am devoid of such.

My God, forgive me for the hatred and sorrow I have perpetuated.

Angelic One, I give you all I have, my home. I am propitious that you will rescue my name from this sinful abyss.

I leave you with lofty aspirations, but above all, I forsake of you to raise your child as I should have been raised, on this land, with this heritage, and with love.

Let him run free in the gardens and laugh loudly. Let him embrace all that thrived once on this land, and in this château.

The souls of my mother and father met and united despite all barriers. In heaven, they now rest in the arms of one another. I long to go to them, to be, once and for all, their child.

Our breaths are counted, our footsteps numbered, and our deeds become our legacy. Please accept and allow this to be mine.

Jacquemart Renaird Dartmount

Jacquemart sealed his words by enclosing them in an envelope. He took the love letter written by his father and placed it back into its envelope. He took a piece of dark green stain from the box and placed it around the two letters. He removed his ancestor's ring and set it down on the table. He removed a stick of red wax and a lighter. He ignited the flame and held it to the wax until it dripped onto the ribbon. He lifted his ring and pressed the decorative front oval, not known by most to be a family seal, and pressed it down onto the soft wax, embedding it with the initial D in script. He took another piece of ribbon, strung it through the ring, and tied it around the packet. He pushed the envelopes aside and pushed back in the chair. He sat quietly, looking at the dark wood walls.

"I cannot risk her not finding this," he thought as he contemplated where to leave the letters. He picked them up and placed them in the box, tucked it under his arm once again, and walked out of the shed and across the grounds to the house.

"This, the last time, I walk these grounds and enter this shell," he thought, as he no longer called the château his home.

Before he reached Piper's door, he removed the keys and placed them tightly in the palm of his hand to prevent them from making the usual rattling noise.

He reached the door and placed the box on the floor in front of it and the keys under the door, but barely exceeding the wood base. He softly slid the letter under the door, allowing it to reach barely into her room.

He turned and walked down the long hall and descended the winding stairs quickly. Once through the door, he ran to the shed, leaving the door open.

He walked over to the spot on the floor that he had mentally marked out for his victims. He took the rope from the hook on the wall and pulled it taut. Jacquemart fell to his knees. He leaned forward, stretching his neck out, and let go of the rope.

The guillotine fell from the ceiling with a quick thrush and swiftly cut through his neck at the base of his skull, releasing him from his life of torment.

The once strong and powerful body stayed motionless, folded down into a praying position. His head rolled forward and turned 180 degrees, eyes closed, mouth shut. His head lay on the floor inches away from his body, the distance between the two bridged by a pool of blood.

Jacquemart was finally at peace.

CHAPTER TWENTY-THREE
THE LAST TO BE RELEASED

Piper woke up after another day, night, and morning. She tried to count the days that she had been there, but was having difficulty recalling the exact number.

"The morning of my arrival, 1; the day I got abducted, 2; the day he bathed me, 3; the first meal, 4; the day I did not eat/ found the letter, 5; my last meal, 6; today, 7?" She held out her fingers as she recounted the events and tried to place a number on the days and nights.

"I have to get out of here today," she thought. "I have not seen or heard the keys."

She got up and walked over to the window, still open. The rain started to slowly fall from the gray sky until it worked into a downpour. She closed the windows. She looked through the rain and mist and saw that the door to the timber shed was open.

"Is he still in there?" she wondered. She stood at the window for a few minutes and walked to the door. She reached out and grabbed the handle; it was locked. She glanced down before turning and saw a piece of paper that was not there yesterday.

She bent down and pulled it completely into her room.

She looked down at the two envelopes wrapped in green ribbon. As she picked them up, a large gold ring fell to the bottom of the parcel. She looked at the ring closely, not realizing that it was the same ring that her abductor wore. She dropped the ring back down, dangling from the ribbon. She turned the letters over and felt the red dried wax seal.

"This is the same seal that was on the letter I found," she thought as she slid one of the two envelopes out from behind the seal.

"This is the letter I found." She was filled with curiosity. She looked to see if the letter was still intact; it was. She picked up the ring again and looked more closely at the decorative front. "This is the same crest," she said as she turned the ring upside down and placed it up against the seal. "This ring is also the seal," she proclaimed with even more curiosity.

She slid out the letter that was still sealed shut. She carefully opened the back, breaking the seal. The red shards of dried wax fell to the floor. She bent down and picked them up. As she placed them into the open envelope, she saw the shadow of an object just outside her door.

She knelt down and placed her hands on the floor and her cheek to the stone tile. She peered underneath the door.

"It looks like a metal box." She looked closer and there beside the box lay the keys.

"The keys!" she cried out as she got up and ran over to the door.

She bent down and slid her hand underneath the door, her fingertips barely reaching the cluster of old keys.

"I can't push them further away," she thought as she stood up and looked around the room. The box that lay beside the keys was no longer of interest to her, at the moment. She could not contain her excitement, "Oh God, please let these be the keys to open the door."

Her eyes scanned the room. "What can I use to slide them closer?" she thought as she continued to look. She walked over to the large, white painted armoire. She opened it, revealing dresses hanging on pink satin hangers. She pulled one off and dropped it to the floor. She ran back over to the door and dropped to her knees.

She slid the flat wing of the hanger to the side and behind the keys, easily pushing them through the doorway. She grabbed them and stood up.

She picked out one of the keys and placed it into the lock.

"No. Please let one of these work," she said as she continued to try each key.

She singled out the fifth key, placed it into the lock, and heard the blissful sound of a click. She reached and turned the handle, and the door opened.

Piper slowly pushed it open.

"This might be a trick," she said to herself as she cautiously proceeded.

The door hit the metal box and pushed it several inches across the floor. She stopped at the sound.

"Shit," she thought, "I hope he didn't hear that."

She waited and watched. Her abductor did not appear.

She ran over to the bed and pulled the long gown over her head. She put her tee shirt, jeans, and tennis shoes back on and ran back to the door and pulled out the keys.

She bent down and picked up the box. With the letters still in her hand, she walked out the door, breathing out a sigh of relief, overwhelmed with a sense of freedom that she had never in life felt or imagined ever feeling.

She ran down the hall and stopped at the steps. She looked down and around the long spiral that led to the lower floor. She ran down the steps and to the front door. As she reached out for the handle, she heard dogs barking and running toward her.

"Oh no, the dogs." She turned and spoke to them, "Shhh, here, girls, here."

The pack stopped and barked.

"He is going to find me." She panicked at the thought.

One of the dogs, wagging her tail, crouched and meekly walked over to Piper.

"Good girl," She said as she struggled to place the keys in her pocket, keeping the letters and the box and under her arm.

The other dogs followed suit. She briefly petted them and reached for the door handle again. It was locked.

"I don't have time to try all these keys. I remember this hall. There is another door through here," she said to herself as she turned and ran through the grand entrance toward the kitchen, where she remembered the appliances, viewed from her upside down position on Jacquemart's back.

She reached the kitchen, and the door was open. She ran out and past the open kennels. She followed the stone path that had always sounded approaching people.

She noticed the stranger's truck beside the timber shed. She ran toward it and crouched down as she reached the window of the shed.

Still crouching, she made her way to the truck. She pulled the handle and opened the door. She placed the letters and metal box on the seat. "Where are the keys?" She looked in the ignition, then the seat, then the floor, and under the seat. She moved out from the driver side door and looked into the bed. It was stained red with dried blood, thick in the areas where the ridges of the metal indented.

"The shed," she thought as she crept toward the open door. She stopped and ran around the other side of the building so that she could peek through without having to stand out in the open, past the span of the open door.

She placed her back against the outside and looked down. She was breathing hard, yet tried to hold her breath. She saw blood on the outside wood of the shed.

She leaned forward and peeked around the door.

She jumped and gasped as she saw her abductor's head on the floor.

She stood still, no longer afraid of being recaptured.

She looked beyond his head and to his body still in a praying position.

"Oh my God, what happened?" she wondered as she stepped into the shed.

She looked at his body, the blood, his head. She saw the huge blade that lay against his shoulders. She followed the rope that ascended to the ceiling and through a pulley, and then hung to the ground.

"He cut off his own head?" Piper was conflicted as to which emotion to feel. She felt rapturous, yet sad, as if she had lost someone she knew.

"Is this how he killed those women?" she wondered as she continued to look around. She saw two holes in the ground. She slowly walked over to them, afraid of what she might find.

She gasped and looked away once she saw the heads of the two women.

She looked at the top of the small table and saw the truck keys.

She stepped slowly, walking past Jacquemart's head and around the body and severed decomposing heads. She held her nose. She looked down at his eyes and thought, "His face looks peaceful."

Piper could not control her compassionate spirit, her natural love for others. Her eyes filled with tears, although she was viewing a horrific burial ground where suffering had occurred.

She felt she had come to know the stranger, and could feel for his anguish. She knelt down and reached out to his head. She placed her hand on top of his hair. His head was not bloody. "I am sorry for your pain and suffering," she said to Jacquemart as she cried for him. "I pray you are at peace now. Thank you for releasing me," she said to him as she lifted her hand off his head and stood up.

Piper was aware that he had allowed her to go free. She was not sure why, but she was thankful.

She picked the keys up off the table and walked out the door, closing it behind her.

She walked over to the truck and sat down on the seat, placed the keys in the ignition and turned them, holding her breath again, "Please be the right keys," she thought. Then, the engine turned over and the truck started.

She placed it in drive and pressed the gas. She followed the road, not looking back. She found herself compelled to view the large grey structure that she came to admire. She looked back to see the roof line before it sank behind the hill.

Piper followed the road until it linked up to the main highway. She followed the main highway until she recognized the signs, "Paris, l'aéroport Charles de Gaulle."

Piper started to plan her exit from France. "I will leave the truck in short-term. The police will find it. I just hope I don't get pulled over before I get there. How am I going to get out of here? I don't have my purse, tickets, identification. I am stuck here." Piper started to panic.

"Should I go to the police? Or just leave?"

Piper looked down on the floor. She saw several small purses. She reached down while trying not to swerve the truck and bring attention to herself.

She picked them up and set them on the seat.

"These must be the purses of the prostitutes. They may have money, but I still don't have ID. I have to go to the police," she thought as she weighed all of her options.

"I don't want to be detained. I just want to get out of here; go to my house and pack my things." She looked again to the floor and saw a Louis Vuitton similar to hers. She reached down and picked it up. Piper opened the snap. "This is my wallet," she screamed out in joy, "Yes!" Then she thought, "How did he get my wallet?"

She thought back to when she had stopped the rental car at the park. "I took my wallet with me. He must have picked it up when he picked me up." She did not care about the details; she could not believe the avenues of good fortune that had been unfolding since she woke up. It's as if I am being watched over, or led," she thought as she pulled into the airport complex. "Where were the last five days?" She smirked and looked into the rear view mirror. Her personality was making its way back.

Piper was not feeling like herself; she was feeling better than she had ever felt in her life.

CHAPTER TWENTY-FOUR
BEAUTIFUL AND TRAGIC

Piper walked into the airport and straight into the ladies room. She washed her hands and face. She wet her hair and combed through it with her fingers.

She walked up to the ticket counter and said, "I need to purchase a one-way ticket to Philadelphia, please."

The lady at the counter looked at her in a demeaning manner and said, "I need to see a credit card that matches the name on your passport."

"I have never been asked that before, but sure, here it is," Piper said in defense as she reached into her wallet and pulled out her American Express card and her passport. She snapped the credit card down on the counter intentionally.

The agent picked up both and began typing. "It is cheaper to book a roundtrip flight," she said.

Piper replied, "Fine, book it that way."

"When do you want to return?" The agent stopped typing and looked at Piper with an expressionless face.

"I don't care. Tomorrow, the next day..." Piper said.

The agent began typing again. "I have a seat in coach, on the third," she said and then looked at Piper for directives.

Piper replied, "First class, please, and that is what? Tomorrow?"

The agent looked at Piper, "No, that is in two days. Today is the first, Miss..." The agent looked down at Piper's identification.

Piper spoke up, "Piper Bla..." She stopped herself, finding that she did not want to be called by Nico's last name.

The agent spoke up, "Ms. Blanche, I have a first class ticket available for $7,000.00. Shall I book it?"

"Yes," Piper replied, however, her mind was on the date.

She was trying to figure out how long she had been at the château.

"Do you have any checked baggage?" The agent interrupted Piper's thoughts.

"No, I have one carry on." She placed the old, dented, and rusted, metal box on the counter.

The agent looked down as her eyebrows raised, "Okay," she said in disbelief.

Piper took her tickets and box and made her way to the gate. Once through security, she arrived at the gate just in time to board the plane.

She handed her ticket to the agent and walked through the jet way and onto the plane. She found her seat and sat down.

A young French male flight attendant approached her and said, "Do you want a mimosa, water, or glass of champagne?" He extended a tray.

"All three," Piper said as she slid the box underneath the seat and grabbed the water and gulped it down, then the mimosa. Then, she reached for the champagne and guzzled that as well.

The flight attendant laughed. "Do you want more? I see you're thirsty."

"Water, please," Piper said, laughing, "You have no idea. Oh, I have a question for you. When you have time, can you translate a letter for me? I will pay you," she asked, trying to be respectful of his time.

"I will gladly do it. This flight is long and I can only read so many magazines," he replied as he smiled at Piper. "Once I serve dinner, if that is okay with you." He smiled at Piper as he took the empty glass from her hand.

"That is really nice of you. Thank you," Piper replied as she bent down to pick up the two empty glasses.

Piper sat back and fell asleep. Exhausted, fatigued from lack of nourishment, and overwhelmed, she slept until she was asked what she wanted for dinner. Piper ordered and rubbed her eyes. She realized she had taken off and was over water.

"I did not get a chance to say goodbye," she thought as she looked out into the endless sky. "The box," she thought as she leaned over and pulled it out.

She sat it on her lap and opened it. She pulled out the two letters and set them on her lap. She looked at the rest of the contents. "They look like legal documents," she thought as she pulled out the papers.

She saw the keys to the château and the truck. She picked up an old silver teething ring. "Oh my God," she said in disbelief of what she had found. "I wonder if this was his." She placed it back into the box that she now treated as one that housed treasures.

She unfolded one of the old documents and read the names out loud, "Jacquemart Adrian Renaird Dartmount I, Jacquemart Adrian Renaird Dartmount II, Jacquemart Adrian Renaird Dartmount III."

She thought, "Dartmount must be the last name. His name must have been Jacquemart. What a great name."

The flight attendant approached her, "I see you have the letters you want me to translate." He held out his hand, "If I can take them, I will work on them throughout the flight."

Piper picked up the two letters and one of the documents and handed them to him. "I appreciate this," she replied.

Once Piper satisfied the primary needs that had been neglected during the past week—food, water, stress free rest—she had time to look out the window and reflect on Jacquemart, Nico, her period of captivity, and her future.

She did not feel that Nico or the restaurant were her life anymore. Though she felt confident in herself, she was lost as to what her next immediate move should be.

"Excuse me?" The flight attendant said quietly.

Piper turned her head and looked at him and smiled.

"I have translated one of the letters and the document. The document is an estate deed. It is for a very large estate, some 150 acres, with a historical château, vineyards, hunting grounds, and extensive wooded grounds. It was handed from three generations of Dartmounts to one Piper Blanche." He handed the paper back without thought.

"What? You are kidding," Piper replied, certain that he knew her name and was kidding her.

He opened the document and placed his finger on it. He ran his finger down the document until he found the section that named her as the owner of the estate. He pointed to it and gave her the document. "Is this your name?" he asked.

Piper took the document and pulled down her tray. She set the document on it and turned on her reading light. Her eyes sifted through the French words until she found her name, as it appeared on her passport, "Piper Florence Lennox Blanche."

"He must have taken my name from my passport. Why would he do this?" Piper thought, stunned and in denial.

The flight attendant continued to speak to her, "This letter is a love letter. It is the most beautiful letter or poem I have ever read. I took the liberty of writing it down for you. It would not be fair for me to read it to you. I think you need to read the words." He handed the letter and a piece of notebook paper to her. "I have not started the final letter," he said. "If it is anything like this one, I am thankful I have the chance to read it."

He pointed at the letter he had just handed her. "That letter is very, very, old. It was written with an ink quill or ink pen. It's very beautiful."

Piper thanked him and waited for him to walk back up the aisle, leaving her to read the letter in private.

She read the words. She felt the words in her heart and soul, as if she had waited a lifetime to read them. She felt she knew the author. She felt within her heart that she could feel the reaction of the recipient.

"Was this his father writing to his mother? Grandfather to grandmother?" she wondered. "How tragic. Jacquemart, (she called him by name for the first time), my captor, inherited a life of misery." Piper felt empathetic, for she knew he had taken his own life.

She folded the translation and placed it into the envelope with the antique letter. She bent over and pulled out the box left to her—her treasures.

She opened it and placed the deed and love letter inside the box. She shut the lid and placed her hand on it as she placed her hand on her stomach.

"I don't know what to make of this," she thought.

It was hours later before the flight attendant appeared again with the first letter and a piece of notepaper. This time, she saw him coming and looked at him, anticipating the translation. "Well, what is it this time?" she asked him.

He looked at her and tilted his head, "This one is beautiful but tragic. May I ask you who wrote them?" he inquired as he handed her the letter and the piece of paper.

Piper was not sure how to respond. She paused, contemplating what to say. "They were written by a father and son," she replied and stopped short. "Thank you for taking your time to translate them." Piper held out her hand to offer it to him.

He shook her hand and replied, "I thank you for allowing me to read them. They are beautiful and tragic." He turned and walked back into the galley of the plane.

Piper sat and looked at the piece of paper before she read it. "What am I going to find now?" she thought to herself.

She read the letter from Jacquemart, written to her, part suicide letter, part plea for redemption, and part bequeathing.

She realized he was reaching out to her to save his soul, and to redeem the family name by returning to the château and raising a child there, her child.

"We are approaching Philadelphia, the city of brotherly love. The weather is..." the captain said.

Piper realized she had little time left in which to plan the rest of her life. "What do I want to do?" she asked herself. "My heart wants to return to the château. Am I crazy for that?" she wondered, and then answered her own question. "Who wouldn't want to restore it? This is a privilege, a gift." Her mind was made up without exerting much effort.

She placed her seat upright and folded up the tray. Piper was prepared to land.

CHAPTER TWENTY-FIVE
HOMEWARD BOUND

The taxi pulled up to Nico and Piper's house. She paid the cabbie and picked up only personal items: her wallet and the metal box from Jacquemart.

She walked to the front of the small brick house and looked inside the garage. Her Porsche was parked in her spot, but Nico's car was not there. She walked around to the side of the house and lifted the basil pot. A spare house key was always hidden underneath the basil plant, whether spring, summer, winter, or fall.

She opened the front door and felt the uncomfortable loneliness that loomed over their home. This was no longer Piper's home.

She walked into the bedroom and sat down on the bed.

"I would love to sleep, but I don't want to confront Nico," she thought as she lay back onto her pillow.

The house had a sense of change; whether in reality or by conjecture, things had changed dramatically.

Piper lay back and closed her eyes. When she opened them, six hours had passed; it was the middle of the night and her flight back to France was the next day.

She sat up and walked over to the closet. All of the suitcases were gone. She had taken one and Nico must have also.

She ran down to the basement and grabbed some old storage containers and carried them up the stairs.

She pulled all of her clothes out of her closet and drawers. She packed her shoes. She did not pack a single dress in white.

She reached up to the top of her closet and pulled down an old photo album and stuck in it a tote bag. She paused only for a moment to open her jewelry box. She pulled out a chain and unclasped it, placed it around her neck, and secured the clasp behind her neck. She looked down at her ring finger and noticed that her wedding ring had disappeared while at the château. She tried to remember when and where she could have lost it, but she couldn't. Piper could not recall throwing it into the woods when she stumbled into the wooded park that had become the hunting grounds, changing her life forever, causing her to take a leap of faith into ambiguity—something she would never have done before.

She closed the jewelry case and walked into the living room. As she passed the coffee table, she grabbed some framed photographs of her parents, her and Nico, and one of Nico as a boy growing up in France. She placed them in the tote and zipped it up. She placed the metal box and her wallet in one of her purses and carried all of the items to her car.

"This is not going to fit," she screamed as she tried to stack the storage bins on the front seat.

She sat down on the floor and placed her head in her hands.

"I can do this," she coaxed herself. She opened the garage door and pulled out the storage bins and placed them in the driveway. She set the tote beside them and walked out to the mailbox.

"This is the last time I will check mail here," she thought as she removed the letters. She shuffled through them.

Piper stopped and stood still. She removed a letter. It was the letter she had written to Nico.

"Oh my God, I forgot about this," she said as she walked back into the house. She placed the letter on the kitchen counter and walked over to the phone. She picked it up and called for a cab.

Piper sat on the storage bins; the house was locked and the spare key was in her purse. The taxi drove up and parked in front of the driveway.

The cabby called out and asked, "Did you call for a cab?"

"Yes, please help me with these." Piper stood up and pointed to the bins.

"You're going to the airport, right?" he asked her.

"Yep," she replied with heavy, heartfelt emotion. She was tired and feeling the toll of the recent events.

Piper drove back to the airport and asked to be dropped off at the adjacent hotel. Piper checked in and had the front desk store her items until the next morning, when she would leave the States for an indefinite amount of time.

The next morning came within the blink of her eyes, and once again, she was on the move. At this stage, Piper was moving through the motions robotically. She was beyond fatigued.

This time, she checked in at the airport, showered, with clean clothes and hair. She felt unsure of her steps. She knew what her heart told her to do, but her mind struggled with the reality.

She was going back to the château where she had been imprisoned and her captor murdered and committed suicide. "Am I crazy?" she asked herself constantly.

The first class flight to France, in comparison to the last time, was not full of preconceived events filled with romance and bonding. There would be no rendezvous with Nico. She knew he was still in France. She knew the town, hotel, and restaurant.

"I have no intention of contacting him in any manner. This is my life now, and my baby's," she said as she sat in the plane waiting for takeoff. Piper felt the baby she was carrying was a boy. She was not sure if she was feeling that due to her inheritance and wishes from a male or not. Regardless, she was convinced she was carrying a boy.

Out of habit, she reached down to turn her wedding band, and once again, realized it was not there.

"It will never be there again," she thought in a brief, solemn moment.

She reached up to her neck and unclasped the gold chain she had placed around it. She removed it and placed it on her lap. She reached into her purse and pulled out the metal box that held the Dartmount treasures. She untied the green ribbon and lifted it up, sliding the gold ring off; it hit the metal box and clanged from the weight of the gold ring.

She placed the ring on the chain and placed it on her neck for safe keeping, and for a curious sense of comfort and validation of her actions.

Instead of twisting her wedding band now, she reached up and handled the large, gold crested ring. Her eyes grew uncontrollably tired. The first time since leaving the château, she fell asleep without effort. These days, Piper moved from sleeping to being on the move again to passing out and sleeping.

She landed and made her way through the airport. She picked up her crates and hailed a cab.

"I wonder when the police picked up his truck, or even if they did," she thought as she waited for the cab to stop. "I am not going near the truck or the parking spot. This is a new day and a new venture for me."

The Parisian cabbie asked Piper where she wanted to go as he placed her large storage bins into the trunk.

Piper replied, "I don't know the exact address. It is a château outside of Soissons, Reims." She opened the door and sat in the back.

She was filled with fear, excitement, wonderment, hope, and adventure. The cab arrived at the road that led to the park where she was abducted. Piper was not sure whether she would have any post-traumatic stress symptoms.

She clutched the metal box containing the keys, letter, deeds, and teething ring. She closed the box and nervously twisted the large gold ring.

The cabbie looked back at her in the rear view mirror as she fidgeted. He drove out of the airport grounds and onto the motor way. He navigated out of the Paris city limits and toward the Champagne region. Piper watched for landmarks out the window.

Suddenly, she saw a familiar landmark; it was an artistic sculpture of the huge metal frame of a horse. She called out suddenly to the cab driver, "Turn here, turn here," when she recognized the road she had turned off of when leaving the property.

The cab driver made a sudden left and drove down smaller unknown roads.

"Turn here, ah, here," Piper said as she pointed again toward the road to take.

The cab driver drove down the long winding drive, through the woods. She leaned forward, looking out the front window, hoping to catch a glimpse of the château, from a much different vantage point.

She felt like a child when her parents used to drive her to the beach. She would wait, and wait, to see the ocean crashing upon the shore and become filled with even more excitement. Her mind momentarily drifted to her parents. "Mom and Papa, I hope you are proud of this bold move," she thought to herself.

"It seems you have company," the cabby said, alarming her as they turned toward the house.

Piper sat forward again to see two police cars and two unmarked cars. Several men were standing around talking. They blocked her view of the timber shed.

Piper replied, "Pull up and let me out, please."

He did as he was told. Piper had him place her personal items on the ground. She paid him and turned toward the group of men who were not conversing about the new arrival.

Piper walked up to the group with an air of confidence and belonging. "Hello," she said as she approached them.

One of the policemen broke from the group and walked over to her and called out to her, "Excusez-moi, this is a crime scene. Do you have authority to be here?"

Piper replied with confidence, "Yes, I do." She reached into her purse and pulled out the land deed with her name on it. Her heart raced as she thought to herself, "What if they ask me if I was abducted and held here? Why didn't I file a police report? Is that a crime?" Her palms began to sweat and she felt light headed.

The police officer saw the color in her face turn pale. "Are you alright, madame?" he asked her.

"I am pregnant. I just arrived from the States, and I am feeling a little faint," she replied. "Can I sit down anywhere?"

The officer escorted her by the arm over to the police car. He opened the door and sat her down on the passenger side of the front seat.

"I have some bottled water. Would you like it?" he politely asked her.

"No, thank you. I think I just needed to sit down," she replied.

The officer asked, "You must be his cousin from the States."

Piper just looked at him with a blank stare. He assumed it was due to her light-headedness.

"The attorney over there," he said, pointing to one of the men, "told us that a cousin of Jacquemart Dartmount inherited the estate."

"Yes, that's me," Piper said, hesitant and confused.

"Why did I just say that?" she asked herself as her mind raced through possible exit scenarios.

The officer spoke, "I must inform you, this is a crime scene. It is a restricted area until we conclude our investigation. You may want to stay at Courcilles, a very nice hotel, or another local hotel, until we conclude our investigation."

Piper responded quickly, "I will find a small hotel," reacting to the mention of Hotel Courcilles and the possibility of running into Nico.

The officer responded, "I can recommend one or two for you."

"What happened here?" Piper asked. She felt no alternative but to keep with her prior statement.

"There has been a double murder and suicide. That is all I can tell you. Je suis désolé. How you say, I am sorry." He continued, "I study English at college." He spoke with a degree of pride.

Piper replied, "Your English is wonderful." She then asked, "Who were the victims?" She continued to play ignorant.

He replied, "One was your cousin and the others, prostitutes. We are not sure if there is," he paused and corrected himself, "was, a third. It seems he had someone held up in one of the bedrooms in the château."

Piper looked at him with a mask of surprise and concern. "Oh my, you don't know who she was?" she asked.

"No, we did not find any personal things. Or should I say, effects?" he asked.

Piper corrected him politely, "Affects, with an 'a'."

The officer leaned in, "I am not supposed to tell, but you are family. We found a rental car, with luggage." He looked at Piper as if he had just had an epiphany. "It was rented by an American; how odd." He looked into Piper's eyes.

She felt discovered, exposed, frantic.

"Wow, that is strange." She stopped and changed her tone. "I think I may be sick. Can I have a moment of privacy, s'il vous plait?"

He politely responded, "Oh, please." He walked away and back to the group.

Piper looked on. "Shit, shit, shit. Is he talking about me?" she asked herself as her paranoia mounted.

After a few minutes, one of the men walked over to the police car and introduced himself, "Bonjour, I am Jean Laissoir, the family attorney. Jacquemart Adrian Dartmount III, my client, informed me via telephone that he was leaving you the estate. I have some paperwork for you to sign when you feel well." He spoke very cryptically. He paused and looked at her, "You do have the deed to the land, correct?"

Without hesitation, Piper quickly responded, "Yes, do you need to see it? I also have the family seal." She reached down and picked up the necklace, displaying the coveted ring.

He replied, "Not at this time. I will schedule an appointment for you to come to my office and present your passport and the deed to me. I ask that you sign some paperwork, and I hope to remain the family attorney." He smiled at her and nodded his head in respect of her new status.

Piper knew that she needed the family attorney as an ally.

"Definitely, I will keep you on, to assist me." Piper paused, then said, "I will, do, need a will and a divorce agreement," she said as she corrected her words.

He replied with surprise, "Oh, I can assist you with that. We can discuss the facts when we meet." He held out his hand and presented Piper with a business card.

She looked down at the card, then up at him. "Thank you very much. I will call you tomorrow, once I have checked into a hotel."

He spoke less formally, "I suggest Hotel Royale. It is very nice."

Piper repeated the name in her mind, "Hotel Royale," then replied, "Thank you."

Piper was growing tired. She neither had the time nor the opportunity to enter the château, nor could she get near the timber shed. She noticed that the dogs were not running around the grounds.

"Where are the hounds?" she called out to the group of men. They turned and looked at her.

"They are back in the kennels, most of them." One of them replied.

Piper felt relieved. She looked around the grounds, but did not walk around. She could no longer think straight. She needed to check into the hotel so she could get some much needed rest.

Her body had grown accustomed to the time zone in France, but she was dazed with all the time zone changes she had moved between in the last few days. Most importantly, now, she wanted her baby to rest. Her baby was paramount in her life and the inspiration for the life changing journey.

She raised her arm and gestured for the police officer to come over.

He quickly responded, "Yes, madame?" he asked her.

"Can you please call me a cab so I can rest?" she asked him.

"That will not be necessary. I will take you to a hotel. Where do you want to go?" he asked her.

Piper replied, "Hotel Royale, I guess."

The accommodating and polite officer walked over to her belongings; he carried them, one at time, and placed them in the trunk of the patrol car. He walked around and opened the door to the police car.

He slowly pulled away from the château. Piper turned and tried to see the large gray edifice.

She turned, faced forward and asked, "What happened to Jacquemart?"

A moment of silence took possession of the atmosphere. Piper anticipated the answer with empathy.

The officer replied quietly, "His remains were taken for autopsy, then to the local crematorium."

Piper closed her eyes and said a silent prayer for his soul.

"Can I have his ashes?" she asked as she choked back tears.

The officer looked into the rear view mirror and responded, "I can arrange that, madame." He sensed her sadness.

Piper sat back and wept quietly. She cried in part for her loss—the loss of her soul mate, Nico. She cried for the atrocities in the world, for the abused, hurt, and tormented. She cried for Jacquemart, and finally, for his father. Piper felt his loss the greatest. He felt a level of love that few experience. He was denied a life of elation. He lived as a shell of a man.

"He was given a son who was titled a bastard and hated by many." She openly wept. "He did not deserve that," she thought in defense of the man who had captured then gifted her.

"Here we are," the officer said, interrupting Piper's moment of solace.

Piper looked up and saw a building—a cold, unwelcoming structure. She was torn away from revisiting the château. She needed closure, and in an unexplainable way, comfort that only the château could provide.

"I found myself there," she thought as she temporarily closed the thought process within her mind.

She stepped out of the police car, once again, with evidence of hardship written on her face.

The officer helped her with her belongings. Piper felt like a nomad. She realized the paradox of her travels from country to country with few personal belongings.

She picked up the tote back and looked down at the photo album. She felt encouragement. She thought of her mother and father. "They would be proud of my journey, my survival, my decision," she proclaimed as she proudly walked out of the car and into the hotel.

Piper looked at the front desk employee and spoke in a broken voice, at first, "Hello, my name is Piper Lennox. I need a room for an extended stay."

She knew this was a small step away from the château.

"I will take this time to gather, collect, and strengthen," she thought as she looked back at the police officer who was getting back into his car.

She turned and looked back at the cordial stranger and placed a forced smile upon her lips.

The front desk clerk worked diligently on a computer and then looked up at Piper and spoke, "Ms. Lennox, your room is ready."

CHAPTER TWENTY-SIX
KNIGHT JACQUEMART LENNOX-BLANCHE

Piper sat on the bed and allowed her body to decompress and collapse.

She did not unpack. She did not consider the room for any form of stay. She saw the room as a holding cell, preventing her from moving forward with her life.

"My destiny is Dartmount Château," she said as she sat up and undressed.

As she looked at the storage bins that followed her from country to country, she lay back on the bed and envisioned how she would restore the grand residence, the Dartmount Château.

Piper had already decided that she would not change the bedroom that freed her. She closed her eyes and thought about the room.

She questioned her memory, "Was it a dream?" she thought as she remembered the room. She envisioned the fireplace in its grandeur. She could see the large mirror that reflected her inner self.

"The lady in the portrait, who is she?" she thought as she drifted in and out of sleep.

She wanted to believe that the woman was Adrian's soul mate, whispering in her ear at night, "It will be alright."

Piper dreamt that she was walking toward the window, opening the iron frame that showcased the reality of the world. She looked onto the quiet grounds that spoke of the souls that came before, and at the statues that held still frames of life, when the property was in its prime.

Piper looked out and onto a small wooden shed that stood as a symbol of one man's desperate cry for a mother. The rough cold structure was devoid of any mothering emotions, ironically.

Piper woke up from an unconscious slumber. Her head was still fixed on the stiff hotel pillow. She was aware now of her thoughts. She was now lucid. She remembered the timber shed as a horrific structure of sadness, loss, and tragedy.

Piper sat up, succumbing to her insomnia.

Although wrought with confusion, she remained proud, confident, and strong. She was all her father wished for her. She was all her mother instilled in her.

As she looked into the dark, strange, unfamiliar room, Piper said to herself, "I am in a short holding pattern."

She was unaware of what would happen in the next few weeks, with Nico and her pregnancy. She was in a different country, an heir to a large historical estate. Piper was afraid, excited, and filled with hope.

She rubbed her eyes and her feelings of fear dissipated. She looked into the darkness. She saw her beloved father sitting in the chair in the corner of the room. He was sitting quietly, rolling his wedding band with his right hand. This was a habit she always noticed.

"Papa," she called out to him as she smiled.

He looked up. "Piper Florence, are you causing trouble?" he asked with a smile—that smile that she had not seen in years, since his death, but would see every time she thought of him.

She listened as he continued to speak to her, "If an event is forced into our lives, altering our path, it will come to make sense in time, maybe with struggle, but it was meant to define us."

She began to cry as she listened.

"And Piper Florence, I know you were meant for greatness."

Piper closed her eyes and smiled, revealing, once again, her strong, confident spirit, "I do too, Papa."

Would you like to see your manuscript become a book?

CPSIA information can be obtained at www.ICGtesting.com
Printed in the USA
BVOW03s1730120114

341554BV00001B/55/P